SAKS, Katia. La Rifa. Morrow, 1968. 160p 68-288675. 3.95

Sensual, erotic, and fascinating account of the "beautiful and damned" of Peruvian high society. What Proust did for France Saks has done for Lima. The characters, caught up in the web of custom and ease, are too effete to escape this society. "The good Lord and I make no demands on each other," says the non-heroine. And it is true. The only escape is in sex and death. There is death and perhaps too detailed an account of the mechanics of sex. Yet the style is delightful — and convincing.

CHOICE *APR. '69*
Language & Literature
English & American

La Rifa

KATIA SAKS was born in Lima, Peru. After attending French and American schools there, she spent a year at Chatham College in Pittsburgh. She is married to an American doctor and lives in New York City. They have one child, a daughter.

Between the years of sixteen and twenty, Miss Saks wrote four novels, published in Peru, which received considerable attention from the Latin American critics and public. *La Rifa* is her first work written in English.

La Rifa

KATIA SAKS

WILLIAM MORROW AND COMPANY, INC.
NEW YORK 1968

Published simultaneously in Canada by George J. McLeod Limited, Toronto.

Printed in the United States of America.

Library of Congress Catalog Card Number 68-28675

To Ron

Part One

one

Summer. A dazzling sky. A flicker of sunshine on my lips. Ripples of light sloping down, gently, gently, to where the earth smells of foliage, mushrooms, and mint. Summer. Furtive, fleeting, inevitable.

I was sitting in a corner of the little café, watching a thin slice of sun as it moved on a slow and tortuous course along the wooden floor, watching time pass, minding a little that it did; not much.

The owner of the café sat dozing in one of the chairs, sweat glistening on his face. Finally, he threw a brief sleepy glance at my table and rose.

"Usual thing?" he asked.

I nodded. He produced a tiny cup half-filled with thick black espresso. He leaned forward and watched intently as I took a sip.

"Watery?"

"No," I said. "Quite good."

He leaned his arms on the counter and lit a cigarette and smoked contentedly. His eyes, black under the drooping eyelids, were idle, searching, amiable.

"Not much business," I commented.

He shrugged his shoulders. A gesture of utter resignation.

"Summer," he said.

Indeed summer. The warm hours, calm, unhurried. A delusion, maybe.

"You come here kinda regular," the owner of the café said. "You a foreigner?"

"No," I said, "no."

"You show up Wednesdays and Sundays."

"True."

"We don't get too many of your class."

"No. I suppose not."

"We get seamen, townsfolk, drunkards, that sort."

"Yes, I've seen them come in."

"You from Lima?"

"Yes."

"What brings you to Chorrillos?"

"Well, for one thing, I like the town. I like the fresh

air, the sea. I like to smell the sea. Breathe in deeply, breathe out. It's very good for your lungs. The air in Lima is damp."

"You come all the way for the air?" He seemed incredulous.

I nodded. He shrugged again and began to polish the tables with a rag. I stirred a teaspoon of sugar into the coffee and sipped the bittersweet liquid. I thought, Gypsy summer. Sun today, fog tomorrow.

I liked this little café that reeked of brewing coffee and kerosene lamps. I was growing accustomed to the naked wooden floors, unpainted walls, empty tables, sawdust. It appeared unchangeable, serene, conclusive; the way things usually are after the dust has settled.

The owner watched as I drained my cup. He licked his lips and wiped the sweat off his face.

"Another one?" he asked.

"No," I said, "I'm late."

I paid him and rose to leave.

"Till Sunday," he said.

I laughed. It was obvious that I had become a habit. A day of the week. A timetable. A certain little incident to be expected, anticipated. I thought I ought to remember to tell Pablo, as it might amuse him. The proletariat usually amused Pablo. He approved of their sense of solidarity, their wage-earning powers, their humor. A veritable life-sustaining humor, different from ours. Ours, he felt, was a dull, ineffectual humor, aimed at dissolving boredom.

"Till Sunday," I said.

I left the café and emerged into a blaze of light: Lima. The thrice-crowned city. Gold, incense, and myrrh. Lima. The city of kings. The city of geraniums and dust.

Short, narrow streets. Long rows of white stucco houses. Red roofs. Geraniums in the window boxes. Dust. Graffiti on the walls. The muffled sounds of the sea.

I stopped at the newsstand on the corner and purchased the afternoon newspaper, since Pablo was actively following the regattas. Then I continued to walk along the short, narrow streets.

Footsteps. A street. Another street. And yet another. An address. An apartment. Pablo's apartment.

The apartment was concealed by huge elm trees. I quickened my step, reached the front door, and let myself in with my key. It was an old house, with a great staircase and scars on its walls and a vague sense of decorum. The ground floor was occupied by an unobtrusive old gentleman. The top floor afforded us the use of several huge rooms, a wooden balcony, and a terrace. At first Pablo had not welcomed the idea of such a solitary, out-of-the-way arrangement. He had, in fact, developed his own fantasies about renting a magnificent old house overlooking the harbor, a house with a certain elegance and nobility: a sanctuary. He had gradually become aware of the complications that such enthusiasm would create. His own place of residence, a penthouse suite at the Crillón, had proved highly unsuitable. Thus, somewhat skeptically, Pablo had agreed to sign a two-year lease on this old colonial apartment. He had purchased the bed, an enormous, canopied relic, at a country auction, fiercely outbidding some fanatic woman collector. The apartment had no other furniture.

I hurried up the stairs, a little out of breath. As usual, the door was ajar and I went in, locked the door, and walked quickly through the empty rooms. The siren of a nearby factory whistled. I thought, I'm late. The rooms were dark and they smelled stale, musty. An unfamiliar smell. Not ours at all. I had a sudden compulsion to swing around and retrace my steps. I laughed it off. My laugh sounded harsh throughout the bare rooms.

Pablo was standing, naked, by the window. The sun was flickering on his face and shoulders. He was leaning with his elbows on the window sill, his forehead against the windowpane. The bed was huge, like a huge ship, and the bedclothes were in disorder. I thought, Last Sunday. There was something appealing, casual, intimate about an unmade bed. The photographs of sailboats which Pablo had hung on the walls had caught the glow of the sun and looked aflame. So did the lovely etching of a nude above the bed.

I said, "Darling."

He emerged into the light and then he drew the curtains and the room was plunged into a dim light that was almost darkness. A large bare room with white walls glimmering in the darkness. I stood, motionless, in the middle of the room, and Pablo came over to me, young, avid, tender.

He rested his hands on my shoulders and peered into my face.

"I was anxious," he said. "I loathe this place when you're not here."

"I stopped at the little café," I told him.

"Again?"

"Yes."

"Do you think it's a good idea?" he asked worriedly.

"Why not? Can you visualize any of our friends stopping in an anonymous café in Chorrillos?"

He laughed and said he could not.

I dropped my handbag and newspaper to the floor, sat down on the edge of the bed, took off my pearls, and began to undress. I bent down to remove my sandals. Pablo took my face in his hands and kissed my face and lips.

"You taste of summer," he said, making me laugh.

I was fumbling with my bracelet, but I found that the clasp was broken and could not be released. I thought of the loose gold disks jingling throughout love-making. I thought, It can't be helped.

I said, "What did you do today?"

"Watched the regattas."

"Interesting?"

"Good start. Rather dull the rest of the way. And you, what did you do?"

"Not much. Went for a fitting. Took a walk through the park. Almost bought a painting. A Szyzlo."

"Where was it?"

"Gallery of Contemporary Art."

"Why didn't you buy it?"

"I don't know. I kept thinking of the empty space that would be left on the wall after they took the painting down."

He smiled at me. His eyes were full upon my face.

"How do you feel?" he asked.

"Wonderful."

"Have you been to the doctor?"

"Yes."

"What did he say?"

"Same thing."

I gave up fumbling with the bracelet. Pablo came over and sat on the edge of the bed, next to me. My skin felt smooth, frosty, like porcelain. His hands were moving back and forth, and he undid my hair so that it came tumbling down. I took the hairpins away from him, put them in my pocket, and thought, Afterward we mustn't sleep.

Pablo's cheeks felt like sandpaper and I loved his smell, he was always full of smells, full of naked odors that lingered on long after I had left him. I rose and undressed in silence. He turned on the switch and patches of electric light invaded the room. I crouched a little and the smooth darkness was now filled with a dull glow and slow-moving shadows. Pablo lay down on the bed and waited for me. He lay outstretched across the bed, smooth, brown, beautiful, with one of those fierce erections that sent delicate little tremors through my skin.

"Come here," Pablo said.

I came. He raised himself on an elbow and stretched out his hand and laid it on my abdomen; and then his face drooped a little, his mouth drooped, and his hand stroked my skin gently, wearily, as though it were at a loss.

"It's beginning to show," he said, "isn't it?"

"Yes," I said.

"When will it be born?"

"I'm not sure. Sometime around the end of winter."

"That's a long way away."

"It's long. It's short."

"Have you told Julyan yet?"

"No."

"Hasn't he noticed?"

"He's not very observant."

"Haven't you been naked together?"

"No."

"Do you expect me to believe you?"

"As you like. It's true, though."

"Is he still sleeping with that beautiful creature—that cousin of yours?"

"Well . . ."

"You *must* know. Is he still sleeping with her?"

"Yes."

His hand paused, as though disconcerted, puzzled.

Then it stroked my stomach, my legs, absently, and squeezed the flesh distractedly, unaware of the complicity between two skins.

"It's beginning to show a lot," Pablo said.

"It feels lovely."

"Soon it will be enormous."

"Not soon. In time it will."

"How does it feel?"

"Lovely."

"And he hasn't looked at you?"

"No."

And then his mouth replaced his hand. His mouth was more aggressive. It was all over my stomach. He spoke softly, slurring his words a little:

"Are you sure it's not mine?"

"I am sure," I said.

"Quite sure?"

"Quite sure."

"Whose is it?"

"I have told you innumerable times."

"Whose is it? Tell me."

"I have told you."

"Tell me once more."

"It is Julyan's."

"So it is Julyan's?"

"Yes."

"And not mine?"

"No."

A silence followed. He shuddered a little and fixed his eyes upon me as though he were awakening from sleep. He lay back on the bed and passed his hand slowly over his face. An uneasy gesture, a gesture of longing and alienation that startled me, drew me toward him, awkwardly, cordially, vaguely aware that feelings were suddenly being sprung on me despite myself. I thought, I mustn't panic.

Pablo was staring at the ceiling, his eyes wide open, his mouth troubled, grim. I kissed the grimness on his mouth.

"How far do you want to carry this farce?" Pablo said.

"What farce?"

"This farce."

"There is no farce."

"Why do you want me to believe that the child is Julyan's?"

"Because it is."

"You don't believe that yourself."

"But I do. Pablo, let's not quarrel. I have told you that I was pregnant when I first slept with you."

"You told me afterward. You never said a word then."

"I couldn't."

"Why not?"

"You were a strange man."

"But you slept with me."

"Yes."

"You should have told me all the same."

He was stroking my hair absently. There was a hard look in his eyes. It seemed a little absurd that we should be lying in bed, naked. It would have been more sensible to be sitting in a bar, fully clothed, drinking martinis. Nakedness robbed one of one's aplomb, it made one vulnerable. I groped about for the sheet, but it had slipped down to the floor.

"I believe that you should speak the truth about the child," Pablo said wearily.

"I am speaking the truth, Pablo," I said, my mouth against his shoulder.

"You always speak as though you and Julyan never touch each other."

"We do. Occasionally."

"Do what, occasionally?"

"Make love," I said, irked by his doggedness.

"Like one fulfills a social function?"

"Yes."

"And he made you pregnant? On one of those rare occasions?"

"Yes."

"A dead shot?"

"Dear Pablo, let's not go through all this again."

We fell silent and lay on the bed, side by side, for a long time, naked and obstinate, a little suspicious of further grievances, of our sense of remorse, of sentimentality.

"I find it very hard to understand you," Pablo said.

He was stroking my hair, gloomily, while staring vacant-eyed at the ceiling. He had lost his erection. He had stopped smiling. He was limp, prematurely exhausted. I laid my hand on him and stroked his youthfulness, his boredom, the desire that had withered between his legs. It felt clammy and limp. I thought, No warmth.

"Are you truly angry with me?" I whispered.

He did not reply. His head had fallen back onto the pillow. He was breathing peaceably, rhythmically. Sleep had absorbed his black thoughts, his discontent. Sleep, like a glowing, seductive drug thrust deep into his skin. His body was outstretched on the bed, hugely naked, in repose. A beautiful body, firm and robust, with no signs of softening or slackening. I thought, If I were to wake him, he would stretch out his arms and grunt a little, like a lovely sleepy animal.

I thought, It must be very late, and slid out of bed, gathered my clothes, and got dressed in the darkness, rather in a hurry. I tiptoed to the bathroom and stood in front of the mirror, staring at the vague, impersonal face as though looking at a blurred image lingering at the bottom of consciousness. As I stood, a series of images began to take shape in my mind, as they always did, unpredictably, unreasonably. Brief, involuntary visions of the past that seemed to be lurking in the back of my functional mind and would repeatedly spring forth, flood, invade. I thought, A subterfuge, and leaned my forehead against the mirror, closed my eyes and remained thus, a long, long time, alone in the womblike stillness.

And there was darkness.

And drizzle. Soft, warm drizzle. Falling outside the window. I whispered, "Nanna." Nanna was asleep. Her big head was lolling on her chest. A big dead flower. The Little Prince was caught, face down, on her huge lap. A muffled little voice. *Draw me a sheep.* Little Prince, don't die. Little Prince, come down from your star. *Draw me a sheep.* "Nanna, it's raining." Drizzle. Dewdrops. Nanna's breath was harsh, hoarse, like a struggle. Silence. Drizzle. Shadows. I crawled out of the warm white bed, barefooted, shivering. Hush, Little Prince. I crept along the cold black corridors. The devil was lurking at the end of the corridor, wearing a crimson shirt. I crossed myself and said a quick prayer. There was light in the drawing room. A glow. A smell of leather, tobacco. Papa. Papa was playing dominoes. Alone. "Papa." "Good heavens. What are you doing up?" "Papa, I have a secret." Laughter. Black and white. Dominoes. The smell of tobacco. "I have a secret, Papa." "What kind of secret?" "A big secret." "Tell me about it." "I ate something." "You did?" "Yes. I ate something." "What did you eat?" "Pumpkin seeds." "And what happened?" "*Something* happened." "What?" "Look." I fetched a soft, warm pillow. I held it against my stomach. Soft. Warm.

Huge. Like a warm, huge belly. "Look, Papa. Baby is inside." Mother's shadow crept into the room. Mother's hair was long and black. She was wearing a crimson robe. Her voice was like darkness. "Wicked," she said, "wicked, wicked." Papa's voice was soothing, warm, like silk. "She's only playing," he said, "she's just a child." Mother turned her gaze to me. Her eyes were black, glaring. She raised her arm and the slap fell across my mouth. It tasted of thunder, salt, and dead flowers.

I looked up and saw Pablo's head in the mirror and smiled at him.

He grunted sleepily, "What are you doing?"

"Nothing."

"You were standing here. In the dark. With your eyes closed."

I laughed. I was still laughing when I felt his mouth. He flung his arms around me and slipped his hand underneath my clothes and groped his way between my thighs, and remained there. Warmth. A sudden thrill. I shook my head with a sense of dazzlement.

"Come to bed, darling," Pablo said.

"I must go. I'm late."

"Come."

I shook my head. He let me go. He sat on the edge of the bathtub and watched as I brushed my hair.

"Where are you headed for?" he asked.

"Home."

"And afterward?"

"Dinner at Karamanduka, I think."

"Is Cousin Maya going along?"

"Yes."

"Good God! You must make a queer trio. Who sits in the front? Next to him?"

I laughed and met his eyes. I thought a little and said, "We take turns."

"Would you like me to come along? I could sit in the back. With you. We could hold hands."

"A gallant thought. But we already are a foursome. We usually bring another man along. Tonight it will be an Argentine. I must go, darling."

He held me in his arms. Again the warmth, the sudden thrill, the sense of dazzlement.

"We wasted an afternoon," I said. "Are you angry?"

"No," he said. "Till Sunday."

"Till Sunday."

I ran down the stairs, down the long narrow streets to where my car was parked in one of the sidestreets. I sped the car along the empty streets without once releasing the accelerator. The tall swaying poplars flew past. The wind ruffled my hair and brought tears to my eyes. In no time at all I had reached the gate. The old guardian came out of the *caseta* and blew his whistle at the dogs. He limped over to the gate and opened it, cautiously, suspiciously, with the stiff angular gestures of an old man. He greeted me with his toothless smile, his fatigue, his rheumatism.

I went into the courtyard and left the car. The whiteness of the house shone through the foliage. I walked down the footpath, cutting through the woods, and inhaled the fragrant night air. I thought, I must have a bath.

As I walked down the footpath to the house, there was a sense of perpetual shadows, despite the lamps flickering along the hedges and despite the exuberance of the flowering trees.

two

The sweet sound of running water. A clear, rippling sound that filled the room. The water ran into the bathtub as into a large thirsty seashell, filled it with its transparence, and then the transparence was tinged blue. I cupped the water in my hands, brought them up to my face, and pressed them against my skin. I stepped into the bathtub, knelt, and touched the water with my forehead, reverently, as though I were bathing in holy water. I sank into the limpid blueness as into the flood tide, into fatigue, into an embrace. I thought, They are sitting at a corner table. The three of them. Drinking martinis. Julyan's eyes keep shifting from the door to my empty chair. He thinks that I'm late. That I'm always late. The Argentine—a likeable fellow, no doubt—is stirring in his seat and talking incoherently about himself, revealing himself as a somewhat complicated, bewildering creature. He talks about the complications, the bewilderment, in quiet humble tones and all the time his eyes are watching Maya's slim neck, her profile, the luxurious lines of her mouth. So is Julyan. Watching. She is smiling that vague smile of hers which is her refuge, as though vagueness had engulfed her mind. Julyan's eyes linger upon her face. She withstands his look. And then her face, calm, indulgent, yields submissively without uttering the tiniest sound, without making the slightest movement. A frugal acknowledgment, casual, unconscious. His eyes are watching her face, the curved lines of her mouth, her tractability. He asks her, "What are you smiling at?"—for he must invade the depths of her mind and take possession of the thoughts that dwell within, even the infinitely rare, precious thoughts. She says, "Nothing." His eyes are still watching her. "You look as though you were smiling at something." "Nothing," she says—and the Argentine wriggles in his chair, a trifle uncomfortable, and continues to talk about himself, his neuroses, the lower depths of himself.

I, the beholder, laughed silently and sank into the water, the languor, the silence, and watched the thread of water that trickled from the faucet, the dimmed mirrors, the mist, the droplets that had come to a stop on the edge of the mirrors.

I ran my hand along the fine, gleaming skin of my abdomen. I thought of the living bubble within, coming guilelessly into existence, absorbed in its own little world of tissue and fluid and cartilage. A little fruit, implanted in those rich pastures, suckling, suckling. I laid my hand upon the softish bulge where the fecundity must be, and the thread of water trickled from the faucet and my skin quivered and I told the child, Your first flirtatious touch.

The door opened and Mother walked in, her head bowed, her eyes nowhere. The pearls around her neck looked dry, and so did the lines about her mouth, the skin of her hands. Mother's pearls. A rosary around her throat.

Mother said, "I heard your car."

She sat down, erect, stiff, hollow-eyed, hollow-breasted. The thread of water was trickling from the faucet and I turned it off. The water was getting cold.

"Where have you been?" Mother said. "They waited for hours. They left at last. Because of her. She said she was hungry."

I laughed and said, "Maya is always hungry."

"They consumed enormous amounts of liquor, as usual. She kept filling their glasses. And her own. She drinks her vodka straight."

"Vodka ought to be drunk straight."

"It made her awfully sick. All over the rug. Afterward she fled to your bedroom. I found her lying face down on your bed, her drooling mouth all over your pillow. I had to change your pillowcase."

I looked at her, at the palms of her hands, at her dark cropped hair. I dropped my eyes and she went on:

"Afterward, she stood in front of the mirror and touched her face up with your powder and tried on your emerald earrings. I must say, her lack of refinement is appalling. I don't understand why you should insist upon exposing me to the association of someone so coarse, so ill-mannered. You are well aware that I have a dread of vulgarity."

"She is in harmony with life," I said. "You may think of it as vulgarity."

"I don't understand why you should insist upon exposing me to her society."

"Peruvian etiquette," I said. "She is our cousin, is she not?"

"It would not be the first time we excluded from our society a member of our own family. Her mother, as you will remember, was denied permission to visit the family."

I burst out laughing.

"Mother," I said, "you are an exemplary woman."

"I have a certain line of conduct," Mother said dryly, "and I adhere to it. I simply cannot justify your tolerance. You behave toward her as though you were her—her accomplice."

A chill. A silence. A false peace. A false freedom. The loop of a rope.

I looked at Mother, who sat motionless and mute, her eyes downcast, her lips set.

"Please close the door," I said. "I feel a draft."

She closed the door and returned to her seat. I thought, She has passed the age when things matter. She is like a desiccated flower. A sullen tired face upon a canvas.

I said. "I must hurry."

"Are you going to join them?"

"Yes."

She was carefully twisting her pearls. Suddenly her face crumpled and anxiety filled her eyes. Her voice was like a sudden puff of wind.

"It's inexplicable," she said.

"What is?"

"This situation. You. Everything."

"What are you implying?"

"It's repulsive. Absolutely repulsive."

"What is?"

"The three of you."

There was an acrid silence. I stretched my legs and stared at my toes. The little toes were slightly crooked. My breasts felt huge and heavy. They began to tingle.

Mother said, "I was at church today."

"What for?"

"I heard mass."

My arm was resting on the edge of the bathtub. A long brown arm, quite detached from its socket, lying upon the white porcelain. I lifted it, wearily, and thought, My arm, my limb. The water was getting cold around my hips.

"Today at church I felt a traitor to my God and my religion," Mother said. "I found myself at fault. As the priest stooped to give me the Holy Sacrament, peace departed from my soul, and I said to myself, I am sheltering a snake pit in my own house; what a great and terrible sin, what a strange frightening sin."

"You are sinless, Mother. You are quite immaculate. Why distress yourself over the sins of others?"

"I felt a traitor to my faith. I felt ugly and impure. I felt unworthy of having the Word of the Lord in my mouth."

"Well. I suppose one spits it out."

Mother started to cry, softly, with a thin, hissing sound. She was holding her head in her hand, her fingertips upon her forehead. I thought, Her nails will leave tiny pink crescents on her skin.

"You. My own flesh and blood," Mother said. "It's wicked. Wicked."

"Please," I said, "forgive me my wickedness as I forgive those et cetera."

"My own flesh and blood."

"Please."

"What have I done to have this happen to me? That I should live to witness the moral disintegration of my own child. My own flesh and blood. What have I done to be punished so mercilessly? Again and again. First your father. Now you. Both of you. It's wicked. There is no pride left in this house. No dignity. God knows I have always conducted myself with honor and humility. Your father betrayed the high regard he enjoyed in this house. I endured. You were left to me. I raised you a Christian. I bestowed upon you the dignity of our name. You have violated it."

"That makes me very wanton, doesn't it?" I said, and smiled at Mother.

"When I go," Mother said, "you will be spared my criticism and my reproach. This house will be yours to do in it as you like. All that I own will be yours."

"You are very kind."

"I pray that the Good Lord will have pity on your soul."

"Mother," I said, "the Good Lord and I make no demands upon each other."

"It will not be long before I go," Mother said. "When I go, your sins will be your own."

I looked at her eyes, her mouth. Her mouth was a thin, rigid line. I rested my forehead against the edge of the bathtub. The water was gray. Like ashes.

The room was gray. Like ashes. Like dusk. A gray room, with the grayness of dusk. A white bed. Cool, white sheets. Darkness falling slowly upon the room, creeping from corner to corner, flying low like a night bird coming to rest. Light growing grayer and grayer. "Nanna, where does light go when it leaves us?" "It moves on to light up the distant half of the world." "Why?" "Because such is the Lord's wish." "Why?" "Because the Lord created the light. And He called the light day and He called the darkness night." "Why?" "Because it is the Lord's wish that we should live in light. And it is His wish that we should live in darkness." "Papa says there are those who live in eternal shadows." "Well, well, well. Hurry now. It's past your bedtime. Put on your nightgown. Where is your brush?" Nanna's voice. Nanna's shadow. A tiny light twinkling beyond the window. "Is that where Papa is now? In eternal shadows?" "Now, child." "You must tell me. I won't let on I know." Shadows rising and falling. Shadows leaping on the walls. A small white neck emerging from the flannel nightgown. "Nanna. *Where* is Papa?" "Shhh. Lower your voice. Your poor mother has one of her headaches. You'll wake her." "Papa is dead, isn't he? That's why no one says anything. That's why it's all hush-hush. Because he's dead. And it's my fault, isn't it? It's something I did. ISN'T IT?" "Hush your mouth. I've told you, haven't I? Your papa is not dead. He's gone. Not dead. Just gone." "Gone? Where?" "He's gone on a little trip." "Where?" "Shhh. Climb into bed. Quickly. Do as Nanna says." "Papa is dead, isn't he? He's buried in the graveyard. And it's something I did, isn't it?" "No, child, no.

He's gone on a little trip." Shadows rising and falling. Nanna's hands plumping the pillows, tucking in the bedclothes. Nanna knelt beside the bed. She bowed her head and clasped her hands. "Now, let us pray." Her voice was like rain falling on the garden. "Our Father, who art in heaven . . ."

The water was cold and gray next to my skin. I pulled the stopper up and the water gurgled slowly down the drain.

"Mother, will you fetch my towel?" I said.

Her face was pale and calm, her eyes dry. Her mouth was stiff, chilling.

"I wonder, sometimes," she said, "why the Lord still keeps me on this earth."

Her fingers fluttered about her face, like captive birds. Her eyes were black, searching, enormous.

"I shall find peace," she said. "The Lord believes in me. That is my truth. And my cross."

My mouth was dry. I touched the dryness with my tongue. It felt like sandpaper.

"I suppose," she said, "that when people like yourself lose their human dignity, they do so consciously."

"Quite," I said.

The last of the water went through the drain. Mother lifted her head as the telephone began to ring.

"Will you answer?" I asked.

She left the room and I stepped out of the bathtub,

leaving wet marks all over the tiled floor. Mother came back, a disdainful grimace on her face.

"It's your husband," she said.

"Well?"

"They are at Karamanduka. Waiting for you. He wants you to hurry."

I raised my head and smiled at Mother.

"I will," I said.

I stood in front of the mirror, reached out my hand, and caressed the face that was looking at me with a faint, faraway smile on its lips.

three

They were no longer at Karamanduka when I arrived. They had left word that I was to meet them at Maya's apartment. I lingered a few moments at the bar, perched on a corner stool, curiously pleased by the darkness, the smoke, the gay chattering, the frenzied rhythm of drums. I thought, Masks, and nodded gaily when the man came up to me and asked me to dance. We moved in close spirals, my hand on his shoulder, his breath on my hair, softly, amiably, sweetly stirred, miraculously removed. I saw his eyes and the look of conspiracy in them and I smiled at him. I thought,

I must be dancing like a habitué. I felt the pressure of his palm against mine; his skin was a little coarse, a little old, like a lizard's.

I walked out into the night, a warm foggy night that smelled of summer. I drove swiftly, with the top down, breathing the fog, the rough night air. Maya lived in the old section of town, in a sumptuous colonial building overlooking the alameda. The house reminded one of a labyrinth, with long flights of stairs and an intricate succession of arches and corridors that seemed to lead nowhere. As one went into her apartment, on the top floor, one had the impression of having entered a huge tropical greenhouse. In Maya's own words, This is where my flowers live—and they make a little room for me.

Maya let me in. She was dressed in white silk and as usual, was barefooted. She had loosened her hair and had let it fall luxuriously over her face and shoulders.

"Liliana," she said, leaning over to kiss me, "at last."

"What is this?" I said. "It smells like a botanical garden."

"Eucalyptus," she said. "The fragrance grows on you."

We walked into the drawing room where Julyan and the Argentine were sitting at the coffee table, busily eating. There was a huge pot of steamed mussels on the table and several bottles of wine, all uncorked, in the ice bucket.

Julyan looked up from the mussels and said, "Well, well, well."

"Hello, Julyan," I said, and bent down to kiss him.

He smiled and looked at me with an appraising glance and said with a mixture of irony and concern, "We were beginning to worry about the possibility of your being lost."

I said, "Were you?" and smiled, without taking my eyes from him. He laughed. A soft, infectious laugh, like a sudden burst of daylight in the room. He reached out his hand and caressed my face and I felt the warmth, the gaiety, the faraway tenderness. I looked into his face, into his luminous eyes; and my hands were trembling, my heart was thumping, as though a storm had broken loose within me.

I half-turned away and greeted the Argentine, who rose, bowed, and smiled with his mouth full.

"Mussels and wine," Maya said. "Will you have some?"

"Yes," I said, "I'm famished."

"We drove to the fish market in Agua Dulce to get them. They are terribly fresh. They smell of the sea."

Julyan was looking at me, a nonchalant look, composed, remote, faintly amused; a look that expected to cross no boundaries, make no discoveries. I turned to him, and his eyes touched my face, a fleeing touch, and I smiled at him, at the laughter in his eyes.

Maya's head was bent over a large terra-cotta vase filled with drooping eucalyptus. She inhaled the peculiar aroma pleasurably and then sank into one of the cushions and shut her eyes for an instant; her soft, marvelous face drooped a little, the shadow of a yawn lifted the corners of her lips. She lay there, very quiet, a small rare bird in a nest of glistening plumage.

She said, "I seem to have a natural aptitude for fatigue."

"Fatigue?" said Julyan with a little effort. "I think, rather, apathy. Detachment. Supreme unconcern."

I thought, They've quarreled, and soaked a morsel of bread in the mussel broth.

"No," said Maya, "fatigue. In its purest form."

"I don't believe it," the Argentine said emphatically. "A moment ago, as I watched you dance, I thought to myself—"

He paused and fumbled with his words. His eyes were filled with tender curiosity; his long, white hands were grasping his knees. His pause intimated that a lyrical revelation was about to be pronounced.

"You danced," he said, "as though you had stolen fire from the gods."

We smiled and waited in ceremonious silence while Maya, the life-giver, looked curiously at this pleasant, softish young man, at the rash hope that had stirred him.

"Ah, that dance," she said.

"Won't you continue to dance?" he asked her.

Maya smiled. Above her smile her eyes were indolent, vacant, brooding. Her eyes rested on us, Julyan and me, as if to say, This evening is absurd.

"We are people of epicurean tastes, my dear," Julyan said.

He spoke without gaiety. Without irritation. He filled his glass and raised it to his lips, and regarded us with the air of a patron who is enjoying his displeasure.

Maya looked around the room, at the three faces gazing at her, and began to smile. She flung her body forward, rose, moved on to an imaginary dance floor, and thrust her head backward and parted her lips:

"Lights on."

She tilted her head sideways, as though listening for a celestial tune, and smiled to herself as we sat in the dimness, in the silence. As the first chords from the sweet silence reached her ears, she advanced toward us with assured, complacent strides and confronted us, smooth, slender, defiant. I thought, Like an African cat.

Suddenly, a rich metallic thrill ran through her limbs; her long, fragile body gave in, soothingly at first, decorously, like a sleeper who is still filled with lethargy. She danced reverentially, thankful for those moments of purity. She sensed the urgency of her body and caressed the muscles beneath the creases of the silk. She danced her dream, slowly, austerely, as though she were willing to endure. But then this mood of tolerance deserted her. A roll of drums convulsed her limbs, and she found herself hurrying toward the echo that filled the silence like a fantasy tango.

I turned my head slightly and threw a brief glance at

Julyan. He was sipping his wine impassively and peering at the liquid that remained in the glass. He lifted his head and his taciturn eyes drifted away, not daring to emerge from their abstraction. His eyes rested upon Maya's swaying form like a man contemplating a self-inflicted wound; like the gloomy victim of self-exposure. I thought, A trick.

I turned to the Argentine and caught sight of his dark, wide-open eyes. His face had assumed an anguished expression; he was crouching with clenched fists, rigid thighs, agonized eyes. He devoured the flesh that had aroused his desires, and a shiver rippled down his body. He inhaled the gusts of sensuality that reached him through the mist flooding the room. A grimace distorted his thin triangular face. I thought, A handsome brute; in a moment he will lose hold of himself; he will sit there, in silence, and have an orgasm.

Maya had captured the phantom she had been pursuing. She thrust out her body and plunged into her conquest, possessed by the urge to placate herself. She fell to her knees, her face a mask of quivering whiteness, her thighs wide apart, her mouth like a crushed flower. Having journeyed too far into the pleasure of dancing, her body quivered, stiffened, and came to rest. She raised her arms and remained thus, as though she had crucified herself. And then she made a little mournful sound, and her body crumpled and remained motionless.

The Argentine clapped loudly. His face was transfixed,

his body poised like a breaking wave. We sat quietly, discreetly, our eyes lingering on Maya's back, her long sinewy arms, her lowered eyelids. And then Julyan rose and moved across the room. His voice startled us, as it came in an acrid gust from the far end of the balcony.

"I'll be out in the garden," he said.

There was silence around us.

We let ourselves slip backwards into silence, quietly, contentedly, until the moment passed, and the Argentine's voice bubbled to the surface.

"It is late," he said. "I ought to leave."

Maya lifted her head and smiled at him: a tired moonflower. She walked with him to the door.

"You are an extraordinary creature," the Argentine said, "the celebrant of a mystical faith."

He reached out a hand and clasped Maya's wrist and kissed the palm of her hand. A little flame was burning in his eyes. He stood there a moment longer, leaning forward, holding Maya's hand upside down, gripping it by the wrist. At last he left.

Maya closed the door gently and began to move about the room, drawing the curtains, closing the shutters, blowing out the candles. The flowers already smelled of yesterday. She carried the earthenware vases out onto the balcony.

"Look," she said, "you can see them breathe the night air."

I followed her along the corridor and into her room.

She leaned over her bed and pulled down the bedclothes, revealing her dolls, tiny and fragile, lying peacefully on their backs with their chalk-white faces and red cheeks against the pillows. Gazing at them with an expression of amused tolerance, she laughed silently.

"They have been asleep since early afternoon," she said, and slid a hand lightly over the fair, angelic faces.

"You know," I said, "I almost expect them to open their eyes and wink at me."

She eyed me with a quizzical smile and drew up the covers. She looked at me in silence while she undressed. She slipped on a wrap and walked over to the mirror and flung her hair back. She contemplated herself with an expression of mingled anxiety and delight.

"I never know whether it is myself I'm looking at, or someone like myself," she said, addressing her image in the mirror. Then she turned abruptly and darted onto the balcony and came back carrying handfuls of white flowers.

"Narcissus," she said.

"Lovely. What are they for?"

"A wreath."

"Another one?"

"This one," she said, "will be the last."

"You always say that," I said with a laugh.

I sank into a chair and closed my eyes and massaged my eyelids, gently, tiredly. The room smelled of flowers and mist and the emptiness one feels in dreams. Mist. Languor. Clusters of tiny white flowers.

And candles. Tall, white candles with fierce little flames curling and swirling. A chilly draft seeping from underneath the door. Maya's teeth were chattering. Her eyes were swollen. She was clutching a small wreath made of tiny white flowers. The petals were tearing loose and falling to the floor. I said, "The petals are falling off." Nanna said, "Hush." Maya said she had a stomach-ache. She began to cry. Whispers and flowers. Darkened windows and shadows. The hammer blows pierced the silence. Thud-thud-thud. Maya cried out, "Stop! Make it stop!" Silence. Thud-thud-thud. I said, "They are nailing down the coffin, aren't they, Nanna?" Nanna said, "Hush. Hush." Mother came over to us, knelt, and hugged Maya to her. She spoke to me over Maya's shoulder, "You'll be a comfort to your little cousin, won't you?" Mother was dressed in a black cloak and veil; her cheeks and lips were delicately rouged. They were all dressed in black cloaks and veils and were floating about the room, grave and silent, like ghosts. I could hear the murmur of their voices. Someone said, "Nanna, you may bring the child in." Nanna crossed herself and took Maya's hand. "Maya, come here, child." "Maya, say goodby to your father." "Kneel down, dear child, cross yourself." Maya curtsied and knelt. She was clutching the wreath. I said, "May I, too? May I say goodby to Uncle?" Maya lifted up her little veil. She said, "I want to *see* him." I said, "He is inside the coffin, isn't he, Nanna?" "Hush, hush." And then, suddenly, someone was standing outside, pounding on the window. Pounding. Pounding. The blows thudded in our ears. We turned around and through the glass caught a glimpse of who it was. She had lifted her veil and her face was white. Like chalk. Her fists were moving wildly, pounding on the window. Her mouth was open. Maya was clutching the wreath. Tiny white petals were strewn all over the floor. Maya's face looked funny. Her mouth was jerking. "That's Mother," she said, "she did the same thing this morning." Her voice sounded funny; like cool water, like darkness. I said, "Won't she stop pounding?" Someone drew the curtains and bolted the door. I heard the click. I heard footsteps and an indignant murmur of voices. The pounding on the window eased a little. I listened a moment longer and then I heard nothing. I said, "They won't let her in, will they, Nanna?" "Hush your mouth." "Will they let her in, Nanna?" "Hush." "I know why they won't let her in." "You keep quiet now." "It's because she ran away with the schoolmaster, isn't it?" I saw Maya jump forward. Her clenched fist was all over my mouth. I felt my teeth cutting through my lips. It tasted warm. Maya was crying out, "Liar. Liar. Liar."

45

Maya was kneeling on her bed, whistling a little tune and arranging the narcissus in tiny white clusters. Her posture reminded one of a Tahitian woman kneeling down on one of Gauguin's beaches. I told her so.

"The Gauguin women are odd creatures," she said. "They are lovely."

"Julyan tells me that I am an odd creature."

"Odd?"

"Laughable. Which he says is somewhat euphemistic for absurd."

I smiled at her. Her face was hidden underneath her hair. I could see the nape of her neck, supple, smooth, and her tiny earlobes.

"Julyan has a horror of the absurd," she said.

I rose and walked over to the balcony. The vines were everywhere. Their long thin stems had spread along the ground and climbed up the walls and invaded the balcony. Outside the window, the tree-lined alameda was enveloped in the lingering darkness.

"Maya," I said, as I walked back into the room, "it's terribly late."

"Don't go," she said. "I'll play the guitar for you."

I shrugged and took off my shoes and lay down on the bed. Darkness disintegrated into tiny fragments. I lit a cigarette. My mouth was full of smoke.

"What shall I play?"

"*Sandunga,*" I said.

Her fingertips touched the strings with exquisite delicacy. Her voice swayed gently, serenely, like a small lantern in the breeze. I listened to the subtle nuances, the amorous words, for what seemed an infinitude of time.

Ay, Sandunga,
Sandunga, mamá por Dios,
Sandunga no seas ingrata,
Mamá de mi corazón.

Dawn, almost. Tranquillity. The passing shadows. Maya's white fingertips upon the strings. My mouth full of smoke.

Antenoche fuí a tu casa,
muchos golpes dí al candado;
tu no sirves para amores,
tienes el sueño pesado.

And then she drew a deep breath and her voice vanished into the shadows.

Ay, Sandunga . . .

She stretched out a hand and touched the strings. A dying sound. I lifted my head and saw her face. I saw her eyes. The yearning. The fatigue. The futility. I saw the shadows about her mouth. And I knew, without seeing him, that Julyan had opened the door and entered the room; that he was standing near us, within reach, among dolls and candles and flowers.

four

Outside—the grace and tranquillity of dawn, the elusive streaks of light, the garden's edge.

Maya was kneeling on the bed. Her fingertips fluttered a moment longer before abandoning the strings. A limp expression came into her face as Julyan walked across the room with his long, silent stride. I looked at his eyes, his idle, impudent smile, the gleam of amusement on his face. I thought, The end of a long, long road.

His fingers touched my face, listlessly, absent-mindedly. I turned my head and touched his fingers with my lips.

"It's dawn," I said.

He turned to Maya and eyed her without rapture. Without indifference. He leaned on the bed, laid a hand on her shoulder, and looked at her intently, as though he could no longer believe what existed in the flesh, only what lay beneath the depth of her eyes, the unspoken words.

"Hail, Salome," he said.

Maya started out of her weariness. Her expression changed as she felt the pressure of his hand on her shoulder. Her eyes—bare, haunted, lost—searched Julyan's.

"Bring me Julyan's head on a platter," she said, and there was a nervous edge to her voice.

Julyan's eyes were intent upon her face. She withstood his look a moment longer, but then she closed her eyes, exhausted by the effort of looking him in the face. He smiled, a faint, ironic smile that made no attempt to conceal the delight he derived from watching her engage in a struggle against herself. I thought, A trap.

"Maya," he said, "open your eyes and look at me."

He leaned toward her, lifted her head from the pillow, and clasped it in his hands.

"Open your eyes," he said—and her eyes opened wide, enormous, her lips opened, and she uttered a faint cry.

"Maya," Julyan said, "you have been forbidden—"

"No."

"—to dance in front of strangers—"

"No."

"—who gloat over you."

"I danced," Maya said, with a solemn, sulky look in her eyes, "for the pleasure of dancing."

"My dear," Julyan said, "you were showing off like a chorus girl. Wasn't she, Liliana?"

I sat up and smiled at him and crushed my cigarette in the ashtray. The bedside rug felt damp against my bare feet. There were ashes on my lips, on my fingertips.

"Maya," Julyan said kindly, as though speaking to a child, "you are about to be judged. Rightly."

She shrank away, suddenly on guard, and eyed him with mistrust. But the sense of defiance prevailed; she shrugged and continued to look at him with cold, impertinent eyes. He leaned over her, still smiling. He grasped her long shocks of hair and twisted them into a thick, luxurious rope that he wound around her throat. She gasped. Her hands caught his wrists as she strained to free herself.

"Wicked little creature," Julyan said sweetly. "Wicked little bitch. Isn't she, Liliana?"

"Please," I said.

"A bitch," he said, "among bitches."

Maya was struggling to push him away and free herself. She jerked her head from side to side in a violent effort to escape. I thought, The old instinct. She fought him with eyes wide open and teeth clenched, and her body rippled and rose against him in short furious waves. She made a claw of her hand and struck at his face and missed. He smiled at her and held her fast. He tightened the knot around her throat so brutally that she gasped for breath, and her hands flew to her sides, clutching the air.

She felt his urgency. His will. Hers was no longer existent. Her body remained tense and motionless a moment longer and then it softened; it lost its fierceness, its resolve. Her head rolled back and yielded submissively. Her neck gave in like a broken stem and her head hung heavy, a dead weight in his hands. A crimson flush was spreading about her face and her breath made a thin hissing sound.

"Julyan," I cried, "she's suffering."

"Nonsense," he said placidly. "She needs someone to initiate her into the art of suffering."

"Her head!" I cried.

"Yes," he mused, "a rare, inscrutable head, isn't it?"

"Enough!"

I turned my head and saw his eyes. They were fixed upon her, bold, transparent, untroubled. I saw his face. A face that could be as rigidly ascetic as it could be charming, voluptuous. A naked face. Deeply stirring. I dropped my eyes.

There was silence, and the glare of dawn. I lay back on the bed, quite still, my arms and legs outstretched on the white sheet. I thought, A stone effigy, alone, forgotten, eternal.

"Look at her eyes, Liliana," Julyan was saying. "Eyes like a statue's, remote, unloving. Eyes without pupils."

He relaxed his grip, suddenly, and let her go. Maya sank down on the bed, gasping, quite out of breath. Her mouth opened wide and she swallowed a large mouthful of air. She breathed as a young healthy animal breathes: as though it had just entered upon life. She flung out her arms and the wrap slid off her shoulders, baring her silken skin, the rich softness of her flesh where her breasts began to swell.

She remained outstretched on the bed, her eyes closed, her face curiously still. Silence fell for a long while. Then her eyes opened with a flicker and the slightest smile lifted the corners of her lips. She sat up. Her hands fluttered to her sides and she started to gather the clusters of flowers. The petals had torn loose and were strewn all over the bed. She cupped them in her hands and stretched out her arms to Julyan.

"Narcissus," she said.

She closed her eyes and a faint moisture appeared at the corner of her eyelids. He buried his face in the hollow of her palms, and when he raised his head there were petals in his mouth and a gleam had come into his eyes. His mouth was urgent, alive. I thought, The Host.

My head was throbbing violently, my whole body was throbbing, my hands felt cold and clammy. Maya touched my face with her fingertips, and I inhaled the musty smell of flowers.

"Liliana is asleep," she said.

"No," I said.

"Aren't you asleep, Liliana?"

"No."

The sun was pale beyond the haze. A dove-colored light had crept into the room. There was a breeze that smelled of dampness, of morning.

"Look," I said, "it's daylight."

Maya lay down on the bed, limp, exhausted. She buried her head in the pillow and closed her eyes.

"I want to sleep," she said, smiling at her dolls.

The hazy leaden light made the familiar images look strange. It lingered on Maya's head, on her closed eyelids, like mist. Julyan moved noiselessly toward the balcony and drew the curtains.

"I miss the sea," Maya said, her voice already drifting into silence.

I smoothed the pillows and drew up the bedclothes. I took her dolls away and laid them on the divan, where she could see them.

"The sea," Maya mused, "the vast heat upon sea and sand."

"We could drive to the seashore later today," Julyan said. "Couldn't we, Liliana?"

"Yes," I said. "It will be another hot day."

"We'll get some sleep," Julyan said, "and then we'll drive to the seashore."

"Sandpies," Maya said.

"We'll leave at noon."

"Maya," I said, "are you asleep?"

"Seaweed and salt," she said, her mouth against the pillow.

We switched off the lamps and looked around us, at the gray serenity of the room waiting wearily for morning, at the white haze that had already begun to filter through the curtains. I thought, Like mourning veils.

We closed the door gently. And left her.

five

The house was enveloped in complete darkness. I groped my way up the enormous marble staircase, holding onto the balustrade, feeling the steps cautiously with my bare feet. As I reached the landing my eyes sought the silver blotch of the skylight above my head. I thought, It's like emerging from a womb.

A door creaked faintly and Mother appeared on the threshold, blurred, amorphous, wearing a white dressing gown like a white shroud.

"Liliana?"

She walked toward the head of the stairs, stiff, impassive, clutching her gown close under her chin. She reached out an arm and held onto the balustrade as though she were losing her balance. Her presence was almost ethereal in the ashen light; rather like a puff of smoke, like a ghost who was no longer anywhere at all.

"Where have you been?" Mother said. "I haven't been able to sleep. I've got such a headache. It's like a crown of pain clutching my temples."

She raised her hands to her head and held her temples between her fingers. I rummaged in my bag and produced a small tube of aspirin.

"Analgesics don't help me," she said. "You know that. Nothing helps me. I must endure these headaches. As I do everything else."

She shielded her eyes from the gray haze and again clutched her dressing gown close under her chin. Her face was rigid, still; a small white mask.

"I haven't been able to sleep," she said, "I've been lying awake for hours, with this awful pain searing my eyesockets. I couldn't understand what had happened to you. Where have you been?"

"At Maya's."

She was looking at me, tilting her head toward me, with a touch of despair in her eyes.

"Where is Julyan?" she asked.

"Downstairs. Locking the gate."

Her eyebrows rose skeptically. She heaved a sigh and closed her eyes. She raised her hands to her temples and massaged them wearily.

"What is the time?" she asked.

"Morning."

"I haven't been able to sleep," she said. "I don't expect you to understand what it means to lie awake in the darkness, hour after hour, listening to the night sounds, not being able to sleep."

I threw a furtive glance at her, at the lines about her face, about the corners of her mouth: years and years of dark, passive resistance. I smiled at her.

"You should have a few drinks before going to bed," I said.

"I don't understand why you should insist upon mocking me," she said. "You know very well that I detest alcohol."

She clasped her gown tightly and walked toward me, a bit uncertainly, with that perpetual melancholy look.

"I wonder why you always come home so late," she said, "always drunk, and always without your husband."

"I'm not drunk, Mother. And I told you before, Julyan is downstairs. Locking the gate."

"He is not downstairs," she said heavily. "You and I know where he is."

"As you like."

Her eyes met mine and I saw her face, the stress about

her mouth, her weariness. I thought, The lean years, and smiled at her.

"You never should have married him," Mother said, and her voice was chill.

"A very opportune comment," I said.

"I never understood why you insisted upon marrying a man whom society would not hesitate to categorize as an overreacher."

"It takes you a very long time to figure things out, doesn't it?"

"I always questioned his integrity. From the very beginning. In fact, I very much doubt he would have married you had he not been so near ruin at the time."

"Rather a commonplace remark, Mother. Coming from you."

"Apart from that," Mother went on acridly, "you were quite aware that Julyan was a stranger to our society. He sort of fell into your arms. And you married him."

"Marrying strangers who fall into our arms is a family trait," I said with a laugh. "Isn't it?"

Mother lifted her head high above her shoulders. A sudden surge of dignity swept into her eyes, her chalk mouth. She said in a toneless voice:

"It was different with your father."

"Was it?"

"Your father was never an extremely wealthy man."

"No. I agree. He wasn't."

"But we were equals. He belongs to our society."

"And a few others, as well," I said, with a short, dry laugh.

Her eyes opened wide and she gave a violent start. "Hush," she said. "What I'm trying to say is that your father is not a parvenu. He did not usurp a place in our society. He was *born* into it. Like you and me."

"And that, I suppose, is your ultimate truth," I said, and stared her full in the face.

She was looking at me, tilting her head toward me, and her eyes were dim, wide open, and a little crazed. Then she clasped her gown tightly about her and walked past me, moving on toward the gallery. She was breathing rapidly as she entered the room, and there were two feverish spots on her cheeks. Her eyes were colorless.

"Come," she said.

I followed her to the threshold. The room beyond was plunged in darkness. A dull, sedate darkness that exhaled a faint mildewy odor. Odors of the past blended with the scent of the flowering trees that grew close against the house. Mother turned on the switch and the great crystal chandelier glittered; the room turned yellow. A grim, egg-yellow room, completely devoid of shadow. My eyes throbbed and I shielded them from the sudden brightness.

Mother was standing before the enormous portraits that cluttered the walls. She tilted her head and assumed an air of hauteur as she regarded the portraits with a thin-lipped, white smile. Her hands were folded as though in prayer; her eyes were ecstatic, reverent.

"Look at their faces," she said.

The portraits seemed to be gazing into vacancy. Solitude and pride had been preserved in their pallid aristocratic faces. Their eyes had never lost their human dignity, their decorum; their faces had never shed their masks.

"A long line of men and women who were born and lived nobly," Mother said, "and you—in whom it all ends."

The portraits, serene and ageless in their frames, assumed expressions of blank obstinacy. They glanced at us with drawn expressions, burdened by the responsibility of a confrontation. I thought, They have escaped the grasp of time; they have become extinct, except as objects to be regarded and appreciated in silence.

Mother stretched out her arm and touched the dust-gathering frames with her fingertips.

"I come here often," she said. "I like to be with them, talk to them. Sometimes they talk back. They are very comforting."

She walked toward a large empty space on the far wall. Her features sagged as though she were exhausted, her hands rose shakily to her sallow cheeks.

"Your father's portrait was to have hung there," she said.

She paused and her mouth drooped. Her face was a little convulsed as she stood before the large empty patch on the wall.

"He would have made a remarkable portrait," she added with a sort of regret.

I laughed. I felt her staring eyes upon my face.

"I don't expect you to sympathize with me," she said. "I have never expected anyone to sympathize with me."

"It's a very amusing image," I said.

"What is?"

"Father's portrait against the wall: flanked by those two arbitrary bitches."

"You have acquired a taste for vulgarity," Mother said coldly. "The Lord knows how hard I have tried to raise you in the old tradition."

"I think nothing whatever of tradition, one way or another."

"Julyan's influence, no doubt," she said.

She stood against the wall, quivering and breathing rapidly. An agonized expression had come into her eyes, her mouth was twitching. She whirled and raised her arm and struck the empty patch on the wall with her fist. The patch that was to have held my father's portrait. Her voice mounted toward something like a groan. A word, maybe. At first it was shock, pain. Then it was just sound.

I looked at her back, her shoulders. Her shoulders were trembling slightly. Her eyes were shut. She was making a strenuous effort to recover her composure. Her face was that of a child aghast at her own temerity. A shy, nervous child, in a huge yellow room.

Bright yellow. Sunshine pouring in through the portico. Mirrors and crystals catching the light and breaking it into splinters. A small, sunny reflection in the mirror, dressed in white organza embroidered in silk and tied at the back with a glowing white sash. A white-silk prayer book. A silver rosary. Nanna said, "Lord, child. You've been in front of that mirror for hours." The quickening instinct of a female child: shy, subtle, deep-rooted. "Nanna, am I beautiful?" "Beautiful is as beautiful does. Come along. We shall be late to church." "I want Mother to see me." "Your poor mother is sick in her bed. She's got one of her headaches. We mustn't disturb her." "Please, Nanna. I want her to see me." "Very well, then. Come along. But we must hurry." The great marble staircase. A faint knock on the door. Mother's long black hair was spilled all over the pillow. "Mother, look: a silver rosary." Mother's voice. Her lipless smile. "Nanna, what does this mean? Do you want the child to be late to her First Communion?" A grim silence. Suddenly the sound of footsteps mounting the stairs. The sound of a voice beyond the room. Calling my name. The footsteps mounted the stairs. The door swung open. Papa was standing on the threshold. I turned and ran toward him. "Papa, you've come back." Mother's eyes were two dark narrow slits. Her mouth was like chalk. She was clasping her gown tightly across her breasts. Her voice was chill. "What brings you here? What do you want?" Papa's face was troubled. His mouth was trembling a little. His hands were all over my face. Mother's voice was like darkness. "Don't touch her. Stay away from her. You will—contaminate her. I thought we had agreed—" Papa's voice was warm, soothing. "I wanted to see the child on the day of her First Communion." "You are a stranger in this house. You must leave." "Please," said Papa. Mother raised herself on the bed. Her face was whiter than the sheets. She was quivering and breathing rapidly, her mouth was twitching. There was a crazed look in her eyes. She whirled and raised her arm and struck the air with her fist. Nanna's cold clammy fingers caught my wrist. She dragged me from the room, down the great marble staircase. Down. Down.

Julyan's head emerged from the shadow. He was standing at the head of the stairs, carrying a brandy decanter and two glasses. He was watching Mother with an expression of amused tolerance.

"Good morning," he said.

Mother's eyes were on guard, a little uneasy, a little suspicious. Her forehead was wrinkled and she seemed to be reflecting. She passed a hand lightly over her eyelids.

"My headache is much worse," she said.

She glided out of the room; an absent, courteous smile on her lips. She crossed the hall and withdrew into her room. The door closed noiselessly behind her.

"What's the matter?" Julyan said.

I shrugged. I held out my hand, and he poured some brandy into one of the glasses and handed it to me. I took a sip. My lips felt hot and dry.

"Must you always humor her?" he asked.

"It's her own house," I said into the glass.

He was looking at me with a set expression to his face. His eyes were hard, unsmiling.

"Yes," he said, "of course."

I dropped my eyes and followed him as he walked into our bedroom.

six

Morning had not yet come into the room. The curtains were drawn and all was gray and silent. The soft pearly stillness was soothing, serene.

"So gray," I said.

Julyan walked to the window and opened it gently, noiselessly, and listened to the sounds of morning. The sun had risen steeply and was shining through the foliage.

"The outer world," he said.

I undressed and slipped into a gown and sat on the edge of the bed. Julyan crossed the room and stood facing me, stooping a little, without a word. He was looking at me with those vague, absent eyes of his, the faint smile that narrowed his eyes. He placed a hand on my shoulder, squeezed me gently, gravely, kept his touch there a moment longer.

"You look exhausted," he said.

I held out my glass and he poured a little brandy into it. The liquor felt warm and soothing as it slid down my throat. And a little stale. I thought, A taste of nothingness.

He walked away from the bed and began to undress. His face had taken on a baffling expression of fatigue, inertia. His movements were careless, sullen, as though all the vitality had oozed out of his body, as though his inner mechanism were one of broken wires.

He was watching his reflection in the mirror: the unsmiling eyes, the tiny obstinate wrinkles about his mouth.

"A worn-looking face," he said, bewildered.

I lay on the bed and sipped the warm brandy and gazed at him contemplatively.

"The sea will do us good," I said.

"I was thinking we might stay a few days."

"That would be lovely."

"Shall we go to Ancón? To Laura's?"

"Yes," I said, and tried to envisage Laura's face, smooth and impassive and much made up: the face of a libertine whose youth has begun to vanish.

"Going to Laura's is like escaping into a delusion," Julyan said.

A smile had come into his eyes. He was walking about the room, slim, white, naked, utterly unaware of the vigor and richness of his skin, of the lingering sensuality that freshened his blood. I watched the purity and wonder of his movements, the delicate balance of forms. His nakedness flowed downward through the shoulders, the firm belly, the thighs, and extended to the striding legs. I drank a large mouthful of brandy. I thought, Hollow and form.

Julyan lay on his side of the bed, where the bed was sunken, and I listened to the subtle sound of the springs. He drew a deep breath and closed his eyes. His body lost its ripeness, its sparkle. It withered, almost. I gazed at the weariness, the stillness, the crumpling of his skin. A weary body, defrauded of its own vitality.

"We ought to leave rather early," Julyan said. "Traffic usually bottles up on the northern highway."

I lay in bed, beside him, motionless, spent, half-listening to the faraway sounds, the waking household, the silence. I ran my hand along the skin of my abdomen, there, where the little lump was ripening. A little fish, infinitely alone and serene in its own world of darkness and fluid. I stroked it with my fingertips and it stirred with a queer, quick little throb—a soothing touch between two skins. I laid my hand upon the throb, upon the sense of aloneness, and I smiled at the child.

"We'll leave at noon," Julyan said, his voice heavy with sleep.

I closed my eyes and my head sank down on the pillow. Darkness filled my eyes. Particles of thought that lay beneath the darkest habitable layers of my inner self suddenly released themselves and sped, boldly, throughout the intricacies of my conscious mind. Visions of the past. Memory eternalized. A vast, deserted vacuum where one might lose oneself. In thought. In wonder. In search of things past.

I thought, In the beginning.

A patch of blue beyond the skylight. A large, half-abandoned townhouse, furnished with a curious mixture of elegance and shabbiness. Sunken leather chairs. Brass lamps. Paintings, some of them signed. Brownish wallpaper. A winding staircase that led up to the bedroom. A bed. Julyan's bed. And us. Naked. Together. His mouth. His touch. Warmth. Like warm rain. Like the sirocco blowing from the deserts. I said, "Julyan," and there was an obscure feeling of melancholy, a taste of apprehension. His movements were slow and somnolent in the enveloping heat. His body was on mine, suddenly fierce, drenched in sweat, beautiful. I cried out his name, humbly, ecstatically. "You are so good for me. So good." He buried his lips in my hair and then his body slipped aside and was at rest. My eyes opened slowly and I smiled; I peered at the streaks of sunshine on the ceiling. "Look," I said, "a thousand suns." Julyan laughed. He slid his legs out of bed, rose, and walked across the room to the balcony. He opened the window and the sun poured into the room. "Another morning," he said. A yellow, motionless morning. A morning of blazing sunshine, haze, laziness. I lay back on the bed, on the warm sheets, limp, naked, exhausted. I could hear the rustlings, the early morning sounds, the stillness. I could see Julyan's face, sensual, serene, his body as it looked after it had left mine, his beauty, his self-sufficiency. I thought, A stranger, almost. Yet, in love, I was made to his shape and size. I was profoundly drawn to him, to the sense of longing, the faraway tenderness, the silent understanding of our bodies. I thought, The body I know so well is that of a man I know very little. I thought of the hidden meetings; the anxiety; the moments together, so fragile, so brief; and the strange feeling of melancholy that had overcome me earlier, in the midst of love, became poignant, absolute. "Julyan," I said, "what is going to happen to us?" He smiled; and his eyes, friendly, distant, drifted toward my face. "Why should anything happen to us?" he said quietly. "I expect that, in time, we will have grown accustomed to our love." "What does that mean?" I asked. "Ah, well," he said, and there was a light tone of mockery in his voice, "our love will have ripened. As love always does." "Does it?" "One must let love have its way." "What, then?" "Quite simple. Our love will have been mollified.

Less erotic. But freer. More composed. It will have crystallized in a new form." "And then?" "And then, possibly, you and I will start weighing the expanding factors and the limiting factors. We will start wondering whether we ought to get married." "Will we?" "What?" "Get married." "It's very likely. Don't you agree?" I dropped my eyes and bit my lips. I raised myself on one elbow and groped about for a cigarette. My body was limp and clammy, the blood was throbbing in my ears. I looked at Julyan's face through the haze, I saw his laughing eyes, his smile, his clothes lying on the chair. And then he walked back to the bed with his long, silent stride. He remained motionless a moment, still smiling, and then he bent over me and his hand slipped under the bedclothes and stroked my nakedness. "Julyan," I said, "I ought to go. I'm supposed to be at a church bazaar. Selling trinkets. This very minute." He took my cigarette away, gently, and pulled down the bedclothes and his lips brushed my breasts. His hands were urgent, elusive, scorching to the touch. I said, "Your hands are hot." He gripped me by the shoulders and leaned heavily against me. His body was warm, smooth, thoroughly awakened. The bed was like a heap of warm sand. I felt his tongue between my teeth, his knee between my thighs. I opened my eyes and looked at the streaks of sunshine on the ceiling. The ceiling was white.

seven

Julyan and Maya drove off to the seashore at noon.

My own plans suffered a delay because of my father, who had phoned earlier to inquire if I would lunch with him. His voice had been full of liveliness and vitality, as usual, but I had been conscious of a nervous undercurrent in his tone, a certain restlessness. We had arranged to lunch at Las Trece Monedas at noon.

Julyan raised a few objections. He found my readiness to encourage my parents' egoism quite unnatural. He preferred to regard it as passivity rather than filial zeal.

"And us?" he asked.

We agreed, in the end, that I would drive to Ancón as soon as possible after lunch and meet them at Laura's villa.

I left the house and walked out into the sunlit streets. The morning had passed unhurried, leaving behind the paleness, the tranquillity. The trees were gleaming in the sunshine; the streets were white with heat. The sun splashed into the square and yellow gleams gilded the stone pavement, the towers, the fountain. This was summer. A yellowing sky. A blaze of light. Dust. A breeze.

I arrived at Las Trece Monedas at noon. I knocked on the huge wooden door and a waiter let me in. The courtyard was flooded with sunlight; the trees were swaying gently in the breeze, sprinkled with multicolored blossoms. It smelled of ancient tapestries, anise, childhood. On the far end of the courtyard the windows of the viceroy's carriage were like crimson flames. I thought, A horseless carriage: the carcass of a lost era.

I went in and the maître rushed up to meet me, cool, smiling, his head tilted backward a little. He chatted amiably—the summer, the heat, the shellfish epidemic—and led the way to my father's favorite table. It was empty. I ordered a martini and slipped away to the telephone. I rang Pablo at the Crillón. A voice said there was no answer, and I did not inquire further. I lit a cigarette and glanced through the telephone directory and rang him at the Yacht

Club. I waited a long time and then Pablo's voice said hello into my ear.

"Darling," I said.

He greeted me with a delighted exclamation, but then his voice became a little anxious.

"Is anything wrong?" he asked. "Where are you?"

His voice softened, swaying gently in my ear, warming my skin. It was soft, golden, like sunlight. I kept thinking of our flat in Chorrillos, the darkness, the emptiness, the huge bed like a huge ship, the taste of his mouth.

"Pablo," I said, "we are planning to spend a few days at the seashore. Would you like to come?"

There was a long silence. A streak of sunlight was quivering on the ceiling. His voice was a little uneasy, a little cautious.

"What's on your mind?" he asked.

"Nothing," I said.

"You must have something definite in mind."

"Nothing at all."

His voice became urgent, searching. It was throbbing in my ear like a fast-beating pulse. It reminded me of his lips upon mine, his love-making. I laughed and asked if he would come.

"Of course," he said.

I suggested that we meet at Las Trece Monedas in a couple of hours, and we rang off.

My father was waiting for me in the bar. As usual I was stunned by his youthfulness, his vigor, the exuberance that emanated from his broad, muscular body. A flicker of sunshine lingered on his skin, smooth, golden, almost without a wrinkle. I met his eyes, cool and transparent, like deep-blue water. He smiled and rose to meet me. He held me close against him and I felt his warmth, inhaled his familiar smell.

"How well you look," I told him.

He moved forward a step and peered at me without speaking: a moment of silent intimacy. I smiled at him, at his sparkling eyes, at his curiosity. He slipped my hand under his arm and we walked over to his table.

"You have shadows under your eyes, my sweet," he said.

I smiled and walked close beside him. I glanced at the white button on his lapel, his profile, the touch of gray on his temples. We settled down and studied the menu and made our selection. He ordered the wines, meticulously, skillfully, and then his eyes drifted back to my face. Again he peered at me with his brilliantly youthful eyes, as though he were attempting to satisfy his conscience.

"Hangover?" he asked.

"No," I said with a laugh, "it's pregnancy."

He moved away, a little startled by my abruptness. He sat in silence, with vacant eyes, as though my indiscretion had created an atmosphere of stifling intimacy. His face assumed the worried expression of a man who fears any further entanglement.

"Is it worth the risk?" he asked.

"What risk?" I said, puzzled.

"Your youth," he said. "Think of your poor old father."

We burst out laughing. He was looking into my eyes, sensibly, good-humoredly, already forgetting the uneasiness, accepting the inevitable with a cheerfully malicious smile on his face.

"Julyan's child, of course," he said.

I was still laughing, looking into his eyes: so much like my own.

"Of course."

After that we settled down and sought to amuse each other. Witticisms were my father's specialty, and he plunged into them, amused by my susceptibility to laughter. We discussed our aversions: boredom, tasteless clothes, fog. And our delights: gaiety, above all, gaiety. He inquired about Julyan and Mother, courteously, absently, and I, in turn, inquired about Dino.

He lit our cigarettes, poured the wine, laughed easily, and behaved, in fact, as though he were an attentive older lover. Or a stranger. He remained his usual animated self throughout the luncheon, and neither word nor gesture betrayed any of the sadness or unnaturalness that lay underneath it all. Except, perhaps, his sudden silences, or his one remark (having begged my pardon) that all females were Liliths.

He startled me on one occasion by taking my hand in

his, looking painfully into my eyes, and whispering in my ear with a strange shallow voice saturated with self-criticism:

"You are, after all, my responsibility. Do you accuse me of having forsaken you?"

My hand felt warm and damp as it lay concealed in his. I looked down at the tablecloth, white and gleaming, and then I looked away, searching for a few clever, tactful words that might reassure him, relieve him of any absurd sense of guilt. But then I caught the swift cynical gleam that lit up his eyes, and I realized my error. I burst out laughing. He was looking at me with laughter in his eyes, those deep-blue eyes, cool and transparent, like water.

Deep blue water. A garden. A fountain. The warm smell of flowers. The twitter of nestling birds. Pebbles. Mosaics. "Papa, I'm tired." He lifted me up and held me close to him and I inhaled his warm, familiar smell. My head lolled onto his shoulder, and his face was like silk against my skin. "Are we going home?" "Not yet, my sweet." "Where are we going?" "Wait and see." Short, narrow streets. Yellow pebbles. Sunshine. My head upon his shoulder. "Papa, where are we going?" "Wait baby." White shining streets rolling off under Papa's giant stride. Wooden balconies. Bougainvillaea. The door was locked. Papa opened it with a small brass key. The room was huge and dim and it smelled of paint. The man was standing on the far side of the room, in his shirt-sleeves, in the midst of easels and canvases and spilled paint. I looked at his curly hair, his smile, the redness of his face, his smallness. I smiled at him. "Dino," Papa said, "I have brought you my little girl." "A dainty little person," said Dino, "a beauty." His hands were warm and damp and they smelled of paint. Little black hairs bristled on his ringed fingers. Papa's face was all over the room, all over the canvases. Dino said, "Tea?" I walked about the room, touching the blobs of paint, sniffing the yellowish plants in the earthenware pots, peering out of the window. Dino sat on the divan, next to Papa, and talked to him in low whispers. He laid a hand on Papa's knee, on his thigh: a big, thin hand with little black hairs bristling on his fingers. Papa was looking at him with blurry eyes. The teakettle was whistling.

"Coffee?" asked Father.

"Yes," I said.

The maître insisted that we have *natillas* with our coffee and brought an enormous dish, together with two tiny cups of strong, fragrant espresso.

The streak of light had moved from the ceiling to the far end of the wall. The sky was still white with heat, but the room had dimmed. The brightness seemed to have gone out of the mirrors, the candelabra, the faces. My father leaned forward and lit a cigarette. He brushed a few ashes off the tablecloth.

"Liliana," he said absently, "Dino is developing a touch of arthritis in his right arm."

I took a sip of coffee and burned my lips. I struck a match, once, twice, and lit a cigarette.

"A ghastly business," Father said, "for a man whose whole life is built upon painting."

"Yes," I said, "of course."

"Dino is an artist by taste and temperament. He will refuse to be seized by one of life's malicious impulses and suffer the metamorphosis. He will find it easier to evade the facts and suffer the consequences."

"Is it a question of freedom?"

"It takes on the appearance of freedom," he said, "doesn't it?"

His eyes were suddenly tired, his face was tired. We sipped our coffee and smoked in silence.

"You see," he said, "I—I know Dino better than he thinks."

I smiled at him: a quick, effortless smile. I thought, Cohabitation.

"Broadly speaking, I share his views," Father said. "Otherwise, I don't suppose I would find it easy to understand his principles, or to justify them."

"No," I said, "I suppose not."

There was a long silence. A sense of dimness. A taste of smoke in the air.

"Liliana," Father said, "I have noticed your name among the list of patrons of the Gallery of Modern Art."

"Not mine," I said, smiling, "Mother's."

"Yes," he said with a laugh, "I have a tendency to

get confused. Do you suppose she could be persuaded to take an option on Dino's oils?"

"No," I said, "it would be unthinkable."

"And you? Could you be persuaded?"

"It's much more likely," I said, laughing.

We were both laughing. His fingers were tapping gently on the tablecloth. There was a limp look about his mouth that I had not noticed earlier.

"Father," I said, "shall I advance Dino a certain sum for this option?"

His face had assumed a vacant look. His arms were hanging loose at his sides. He was gazing at the ceiling, absent-mindedly, as though he were utterly oblivious of my presence; as though he had already departed.

"The gallery would reimburse me, of course," I said, and looked away.

"As you like," he said.

I wrote out a check. My fingertips felt a little heavy, a little numb. My father thanked me and folded the check and slipped it into his breast pocket.

"More coffee?" he asked.

Pablo walked in at that moment, looking young, suntanned, handsome. I waved at him, and he walked over to our table, a puzzled expression on his face. My father drew a deep breath and I glanced at him. I recognized the grave, intent look in his eyes, the stiffening of his jaw, the slight grimace that deformed his mouth. I thought, He is not invulnerable. Pablo mistook his look for one of parental scruples and hastened to make some commonplace remark that lacked originality and moral conviction and would have, in fact, proved disastrous had it been aimed at an astute, vigilant parent.

My father seemed delighted by Pablo's confusion. He gave him an amused glance and rose to leave.

"Well," he said benevolently, "I must be off."

He kissed me on both cheeks, shook hands with Pablo, and left us. I caught a glimpse of his face as he walked across the courtyard: the eyes, remote and beautiful, the playful smile, the aloofness. And then the courtyard was empty. Two o'clock struck. Pablo was looking at me with a quizzical expression in his eyes.

"Remarkable," he said.

"What is?"

"Genes."

I laughed. I slipped a hand under his arm, and we walked out into the sun.

eight

Laura's villa was gleaming in the sun, remote, beautiful, perched upon huge sand-colored rocks that sloped gently down to the sea. Pablo and I arrived to find the villa deserted except for the servants. Everyone else, it seemed, must be loose and adrift, a little drunk with sunshine, with summer.

The sky was pale with heat. The trees were bright and alive, rustling in the breeze. Down below, the sea was tranquil, blue, with only an occasional burst of whiteness swaying and rising, causing the yachts to bob and dip at their moorings.

Pablo and I wandered about the gardens. No sound. No shadow. Only warmth. And the sweet smell of earth, the warm breath of wind. We walked toward the flowers, where the sunny little buds were unfolding themselves, turning their heads toward the sun. We came upon the garden's edge, where the earth was bursting with sun.

"So still," I said.

"The stillness of summer," Pablo said.

He bent over me and I felt his breath. I felt his hands upon my face, warm, searching, feeling my skin. My skin was hot and a little moist. The earth under my feet was moist. The sky was pale, with a pallor of summer.

Pablo rested his hands on my shoulders and peered into my face. His eyes were full upon my face. I could see the yellow specks in his pupils. He drew me to him, a little wildly.

"Let's go into the house," he said, "upstairs."

"Here?" I said. "Now?"

"Yes," he said, "everyone is at the beach."

I smiled at him. I thought of Laura and the others, lying lazily on the beach, a little drowsy with sunshine and heat; and us, Pablo and I, empty-headed and trembling, sinking down on one of Laura's narrow brass beds.

"Come," he said.

I slipped my tongue between his lips. His eyes were watchful from beneath his eyelids. The air was filled with sunshine. I could feel the heat, the stillness, the warmth between my legs.

"Come," he said.

He led the way and I followed. His fingers closed gently on my wrist and I felt his touch, the tightness of his body. Time was standing still, in the shadows, in a kind of sleep. Time was slipping backward into silence, into stillness, allowing the faraway images of the past to assume visible form.

Purple flashes quivering in the darkness. The sweet melancholy of a guitar. Midnight. The faint scent of mimosa. I sipped my martini and raised my eyes and looked at them. They were dancing quietly, in silence, in the middle of the dance floor. Julyan rested his cheek against hers and buried his lips in her hair. Maya closed her eyes and laid her head on his shoulder, and they continued to dance, somnolently, without a word, pressing close against one another. I lowered my eyes, rose, and walked away toward the garden, toward the darkness. The garden was deserted. A bit of moon was shining through the foliage. My face was burning. I walked farther and farther away. I slowed down at last and came to a standstill. I remained thus a long time, without moving, without thinking. And then I felt the grip of warm, gentle fingers closing on my wrist. I looked up, a bit startled, and saw his face. A face unknown. A mere blotch in the shadow. A stranger's face peering into mine. There was a faint smile on his lips. His fingers were gripping my wrist. I smiled at his face, at the moonlight, at the last plaintive throb of a guitar. I said, "I have never seen you before." "I have been watching you," he said, "on the dance floor. At the bar. And now, here." A bit of moon was shining above the trees. I could hear the distant sound of marimbas, guitars, people's voices. I could feel the grip of his fingers on my wrist. He drew me toward him, and pressed me to him, and I felt his warmth, his hard muscular body against mine. "I have been watching you a long time," he said. "You are exquisite." I felt his lips, warm and moist; I felt the nakedness of his tongue. A feeling of drowsiness and bewilderment came upon me: a feeling of sinking down into the darkness. I said, "Julyan!" "No," he said, "my name is Pablo." I glanced at his face, his eyes, grave and motionless in the darkness. I smiled at him. I thought, Julyan is dancing in silence, in the middle of the dance floor. With her. They dance well together. She is light and graceful in his arms. He inhales her warmth, her sweetness. He reaches out for her face. He feels her skin, the movements of her body, the brusque gestures, the abandonment. Pablo's eyes were gleaming. He said, "You are exquisite." I drew away from him and made a move toward the dance floor. "The waltz," I said. His fingers again closed tightly on my wrist. "No," he said. I watched the curious stillness of his face. The guitars burst out with sound. He drew me to him, gently, and I felt his hands. I said, "Here? Now?" I felt his hands as they found my skin. I felt the tightness of his body. "Come," he said. He led the way and I followed.

We walked through the gardens of the Crillón, the ballrooms, up the thickly carpeted staircase, along the corridors. "I live at the Crillón," he said. We entered his suite, and he closed the door. His body came close to mine. Again his hands were groping softly in the darkness, stroking my breasts. I felt the warmth of his mouth through the silk. A thrill ran up my legs; my knees were trembling a little. I sat on the edge of the bed, fully clothed, feeling the warmth, the darkness. I thought, I suppose it's inevitable. His hands were feeling for my skin. My skin was quivering. He said, "You called me Julyan." "Yes." "Why?" "I don't know. I wasn't thinking." "Who is Julyan?" "My husband." "Where is he?" "Downstairs." There was darkness, and the touch of his hands, and his teeth hurting my lips. There was the distant sound of an orchestra. I thought, They are dancing together, in the shadows, in a kind of sleep. Julyan's lips are buried in her hair. Her face is calm, tender, and there are shadows under her eyes. Pablo's arms tightened around me. I turned my face toward him and smiled; and then his body was on mine. I sank down on the bed and lay quite still and smiled at him as he lay outstretched on the bed beside me. I could see his long, slim neck, the curve of his face, the blurred smile on his lips. His smell was sweet and cool. I thought, I mustn't wrinkle my clothes. I felt the coolness of the sheets, his mouth, his huge swelling erection. And then, quite suddenly, my body stiffened and drew away from him. I grew rigid, unyielding; contemptuous of the sudden sense of intrusion, of the weight that pinned me down and flattened me against the bed: a stranger's weight. I made a brusque gesture to free myself, half rising from the bed. I seized his wrists and turned my face violently away from him. I thought, A reflex. He remained motionless for a moment, amused, slightly intrigued. But then, his smile, his unconcern, were far stronger than my half-hesitant, half-bewildered struggle. His mouth came near me again; his lips closed upon my nipples; his body, already unclothed, slipped between my thighs, and I felt the warmth, the exquisite warmth, infinitely soothing. A feeling of calm came over me; my rigidity dissolved, my limbs abandoned themselves obediently, without a struggle. My body gave itself; it opened softly to his swollen flesh, and he came into me, slowly, soothingly, like darkness, like sleep.

nine

Sunshine was pouring through the window. The room smelled of sweet violets, of disorder, of summer. A marvelous room, where Laura's latent influence could be sensed in the sumptuous furnishings, silk curtains, mirrors. I thought, A room where any love but pagan love would be inconceivable.

Pablo was lying quite still on the narrow brass bed, breathing peacefully, with a sense of utter abandonment. I could see the whiteness of the sky beyond the window, Pablo's suntanned face, his body still touching mine.

"I like narrow brass beds," I said, and smiled at him.

He did not reply. He was lying quite still, staring vacantly at the ceiling. His mood seemed dominated by a growing feeling of weariness and depression. I thought, After love.

"Darling," I said, and bent over him and my lips touched his eyelids, his eyebrows.

I glanced at his face as he rose on his elbow and groped for a cigarette. A face that had known thrill, warmth, fatigue. Within me. A face infinitely alive and pure. He lit a cigarette and blew a stream of smoke from his mouth and nose.

"Liliana," he said, "and now, what?"

I rose, walked to the balcony, and opened the window. Down below, the sea, the sand, the heat.

"Well," I said with a laugh, "now we ought to go down to the beach and join the others."

"And then what?"

"We'll go into the sea."

"And then?"

"We'll swim. We can go surfing, if you like."

Pablo walked over to me and laid a hand over my mouth. He closed the window, quietly, and took my face in his hands and peered into my eyes.

"You must tell me," he said. "I want you to tell me."

"Tell you what?"

"What you have in mind. Why you have asked me to come here."

I flung my arms around him and burst out laughing. "Dear Pablo," I said.

"Don't laugh," he said, and his voice was chill.

I saw his face bent over mine. His eyes hardened. A dark, unsmiling look had come into his face.

"You must tell me," he said. "I must know."

"Words," I said.

"Yes. Words."

"They are best unsaid."

"I must know."

I drew away from him and walked to the dressing table and slipped into a robe. The room was hot and smelled of sweet violets. Pablo sat on the edge of the bed and watched as I brushed my hair.

"Have you talked to Julyan yet?" he asked.

"What about?"

"Us."

"No."

"Why not? He might find it amusing."

"No," I said, "no."

I raised my head and peered at his face, his half-smile. His face was dim and specked on the antiqued mirror. His eyes were a little disconcerted, suspicious, as though they had grown into the habit of remaining on guard.

"Liliana," he said, "I don't like what we are doing."

"What, darling?"

"The hidden meetings. The lies. The anxiety."

"But, Pablo—"

"I don't like making love the way we do. Hurriedly. Shabbily. In broad daylight. Knowing that we aren't allowed a whole night to ourselves. Fearing that someone will run into us. And find us out."

"But darling—"

"I don't like having to hide."

He closed his eyes and passed his hand slowly over his face. A familiar gesture, clumsy, and a little sad. I dropped my eyes and continued to brush my hair, without answering. A silence followed, and then he reached across the dressing table and stroked my face and lips.

"Liliana," he said wearily, "do you like sleeping with me?"

"Yes," I said, "yes, darling."

"Do you like it very much?"

"Very much."

"And him?"

"Him?"

"Yes. Him. Do you like sleeping with him?"

"We hardly ever sleep together."

"I see. You hardly ever sleep together. A brother-and-sister marriage."

"Well."

"So were Apollo and Diana: brother and sister. Both light-gods, too. One working in daylight. The other in the dark, with oblique reflected light."

"Pablo. Words: what are they for? Please let's not quarrel."

"I have no wish to quarrel, darling. I am simply curious. Very curious. About this brother-husband of yours. With whom you no longer sleep. Or so you say."

"Hardly ever."

"I see. Yet, it is *his* child you are carrying?"

"Yes."

"And not mine?"

"No."

He rose suddenly and grasped my shoulders. He drew my head toward him and kissed me on the lips.

"You are an obstinate little fool," he said.

He knelt and his arms tightened around my waist. He undid my robe and passed his hand slowly along the curve of my abdomen. And then his mouth was all over my abdomen, there, where the child was stirring faintly. I could smell his warmth, the nakedness of his skin, his uneasiness. I stroked his hair gently and brought my face close to his.

"Liliana," Pablo said, his face utterly at a loss, "what is it that you want? You seldom say."

"I seldom know."

"Is it us you want? Both of us? He and I? Do you want us to grow into a habit? Together? Renounce nothing? Take turns in siring you?"

"Pablo, please."

He rose and walked away to the window. He picked up a cigarette and lit it with a brusque gesture. "How much longer do you expect this to go on?" he asked.

"This?"

"This ridiculous situation that involves the three of us."

"The four of us."

"As you like: the four of us. How long do you expect it to last?"

I shrugged and bent down to fasten my sandals. My breasts felt warm and heavy. There was a bruise on my thigh, where Pablo's fingers had sunk during love. I thought, To him, it's like renouncing his thoughts, his lucidity, and engaging in combat to preserve a sense of equilibrium.

"You have created a very delicate balance," Pablo said. "Are you aware of its brittleness? Do you realize that the tiniest jolt, the slightest tremor, is bound to break it?"

"Yes," I said, "I suppose I do."

"It should be amusing to watch it happen."

There was a long silence. He smoked quietly, no longer looking at anything. The sky was white beyond the window. I could hear the sea gulls, a distant siren, the muffled whisperings of the sea.

"I find it very hard to understand you," Pablo said. "There is a sense of remoteness, unnaturalness, that I don't understand. What in God's name do you want?"

My face was white on the mirror. I dabbed a little red on my lips. Outside, the cries of the sea gulls, the sea.

"I want the sea," I said. "I want to plunge into the water and feel the freshness, the salt. Shall we go to the water?"

"Yes," Pablo said. "What else?"

ten

Beyond the dunes—the sand, the emptiness of the sea, the rust-colored rocks, the waves breaking gently on the beach.

"Over there," Pablo said, "by the dunes."

We walked along the footpath that sloped down to the sea and waved at them. They were sprawled on the sand, young, suntanned, handsome, the sun streaming on their faces, on their half-naked limbs. We could hear their voices, whirling in the air, bubbling with laughter.

Laura saw us coming and walked over to meet us.

As usual, she was dressed in pale shades of lilac and her face was lovely, impassive, carefully made up to preserve her celebrated beauty. I thought, She is ageless. She seemed amused to see us and greeted us with a look of cheerful conspiracy.

"Come, children," she said.

We walked to where the group was lying on the sand. Pablo and I stood side by side, facing them, and allowed their indolent glances to fall upon us. They smiled. Laura's mouth was full of laughter, as though it were saying, Look at these children, brown, handsome, disheveled; they just got out of bed.

"You know everyone, of course," Laura said.

Of course. Everyone. Their faces, the sound of their voices, their weariness, their laughter.

I lowered my eyes and caught a glimpse of those slim, naked statues gleaming in the sun. My eyes drifted from face to face, knowingly, unhurriedly. I thought, A summer tableau.

Julyan. Weary beneath his smile. Barely conscious of the glowing sky above his head. His senses thrilled, alert. A taste of sunshine on his lips.

Maya. Outstretched on a heap of sand. Asleep. Immersed in languorous solitude. Her mouth wide open, like an open wound.

Laura. Serene, impassive, exquisitely groomed. A smell of sweet violets. A sense of vanishing youth, fatigue.

Juan-Luis. A summer visitor. (I thought, Laura has begun to run after the young ones.)

Coco. Waiting silently. Unable to escape. Her strong body thrust into a dense slumber. Her large commanding head like that of a sphinx. A hard mouth. Unshaven armpits. A sense of the irreparable.

Sabina. The sylph. Golden, pubescent, pretty. Asleep under the hollow of Coco's arm, her face half-hidden by her long strands of hair. Bluish eyelids. The breasts of a child. (I thought, Coco must follow her like a shadow these days.)

Leandro. The wanderer. The shell. Kneeling on the sand, his strong brown thighs loosely apart. His keen pointed nipples glistening on his chest. His fingers opening and closing on the sand, quietly, absently. His eyes like the chill of morning.

And us. Pablo and I. Brown, handsome children. Flushed and disheveled. The marks of the sheet and the pillow fresh on our skin.

I smiled and looked away from them. The images lingered in my eyes a moment longer. I wandered away and plunged into the sea. I cupped my hands and pressed the water against my eyes, my lips. The sea was swollen, splendid, and I leaned against the waves, eagerly, bathed in freshness and salt. And then the current tipped me backward, like two strong hands upon my shoulders, and I slipped between the waves, laughing, and felt the brightness of the sky, the soft confusing murmur of the sea against my ears. I closed my eyes and a series of images flooded my mind. Furtive, fleeting images. Half-forgotten glimpses of the past. I thought, As it was in the beginning.

The sea at night. Swollen, dark, splendid. The sky was dark, with patches of gray beneath the clouds. I rushed into the waves, into the night, holding my breath, spreading my arms and legs, and I felt the chill of the water against my naked skin, the taste of salt in my mouth. Julyan's head appeared on the surface. A large, pallid figure against the gloomy shadow of the sea. I thought, Ondine, and laughed at him, a blurred little laugh, soft and shivery. He said, "Come." He swam against the waves, naked, with swift, sure movements. My body stirred and I plunged back into the waves, fleeing from him with a wild cry like laughter. I thought, Far enough, deep enough. Julyan laughed and gripped my ankles; and then his legs were tightly wrapped around me, cold and slippery, his hands were holding up my breasts, fumbling with the stiff, icy nipples, and I felt the chill of his flesh against mine, the hard charging movements of his tongue inside my mouth, the taste of salt. We were swept under a wave, swaying and stooping, adrift in a world of water: man and woman, alone after Creation. The sound of waves was gurgling somewhere in my ears, and all the time his tongue was large and warm inside my mouth, his cold numbed fingers were fumbling blindly at my nakedness. We emerged to the surface, gasping for breath, and it was like awakening from sleep. I watched the sky, almost black, and our small fire blazing on the shore, and Julyan's hair, wet and lovely, sticking all over his forehead. I said, "Julyan," and turned my face to him and flung my arms around his waist and again his face was blurred in the water. "My little mermaid," he said. "If I were a mermaid," I said, "I could not make love." "You would spawn. Like the fish." We laughed, and he lowered his hands and pressed them against the soft roundness of my buttocks. He said, "Did anyone ever make you come in the water?" I laughed and shook my head and pressed my face against him. "Well, then," he said, "well, then." My body was quivering, my lips were full of salt; I felt his hands, groping gently, cautiously, and the sea, rising and falling, and then I felt his fingertips, sharp, piercing, and I cried out a little; again and again my body jerked with a sudden thrill, a shiver, a curious throbbing in my bowels. His hands took no notice of my cry, they knew their way, their will; they pressed on among the folds of my startled flesh. My body drifted toward him, weightless, swaying in the water, with a dim sense of wonder, and I felt the taste of the sea in his mouth, and the silence, and the emptiness of the sea.

"Liliana," Laura said, "aren't you afraid of freckles?"

I laughed and gestured no and dipped my face into the water, cold and blue, and watched her swimming with even, languid strokes, keeping her long white neck carefully stretched out and her elegant head high above water. The afternoon sun gave a luxurious glow to her skin; her eyes were shielded by enormous sunglasses.

We swam toward shore together, freshened by the water, discussing trivialities, not really listening to each other. The sun had begun to shrink back a little and head toward the hills.

"I haven't seen you since the races," Laura said. "Such a fruitless afternoon, remember? Afterward, you vanished. All of you. And I met Juan-Luis. At mass. He was lovely, young, and a bit puritanical. A virgin. But not for long, mind you. Such moral taboos are usually short lived."

She laughed. She spoke absently, affectionately, with a slight trace of sarcasm, as though she were addressing no one in particular. We reached the shore, still laughing, and Juan-Luis rushed forward with a towel as Laura came out of the water. She smiled and patted him on the cheek and we walked over to Coco and Sabina.

Sabina was lying on the sand, relaxed, golden, fragile, staring into vacancy, her thin adolescent limbs sprawled over the sand. Coco was kneeling beside her, looking down into her face, talking in whispers.

"You have been so quiet," Laura said to them. "Are we disturbing you?"

"Sabina needs her rest," Coco said. "She is easily tired."

"Yes, of course."

Coco took hold of large handfuls of Sabina's hair and let the dark gold strands slip through her fingers.

"Have you ever seen anything so radiant?" she asked.

We laughed, a little taken by surprise, and turned our obedient gaze upon Sabina's head, her idle, delicate face, her golden eyes. We remained silent, as though in the presence of a fetish. Sabina's face became very quiet and she closed her eyes; her upper lip curled over her tiny white teeth. I thought, One can't blame the serpent.

"I'm bored," Sabina said, tugging at her hair. "Let's play *Mata Tiru Tiru La.*"

"You will tire yourself," Coco said.

Sabina shrugged and started to rise. Coco leaped forward and gripped her by the arm and forced her down onto the sand.

"I don't want you to tire yourself," she said soothingly.

"I want to play," Sabina said, her lips twitching slightly.

She edged away from Coco, as though the contact had suddenly become a vexation. She broke away sharply and escaped toward the edge of the water. Coco rose hurriedly, muttering something, and followed Sabina with a distraught expression on her face.

"Come, Juan-Luis," Laura said briskly. "If they are going to play, we must play too."

I walked slowly past them and wandered away toward the others. Julyan and Pablo were lying in the sun, discussing the regattas in deep, somnolent voices. Pablo's eyes were restless, as though he were looking for someone. He raised his head, saw me, and his expression was transformed. His eyes narrowed and gleamed and he smiled weakly. I tilted my mouth toward him a little and looked away, to where Maya was amusing herself by writing our names on the sand.

She was blinking in the sunshine, smiling with the corners of her lips. She wore that calm, meditative expression that others often found disconcerting. The sand trickled through her long slender fingers, clinging to the moist patches of her skin.

Leandro was lying on his back, quite still, his hands clasped beneath his head. He sat up abruptly and flung an amused glance at Maya's fingers as they moved quickly along the sand.

"Words should not be imprinted on sand," he told her.

"Why not?"

"Because of the water, the wind."

"No matter," she said, "nothing should be everlasting."

I collapsed beside them like a big clumsy sandpie and laid my face against the sand. Maya leaned over and gently stroked my face. I could feel the warmth at the tips of her fingers.

"Your face is hot," she said.

I leaned my elbows on the sand and closed my eyes, shutting off all colors and forms. The sky no longer existed, except as a crimson blur that filled my eyelids. The sand was hot against my skin, but I could already feel the chill of dusk in the air. The child awakened with a start to find itself still in darkness. It stirred faintly within my womb and then was quiet again. I could hear the sea gulls, the soft murmur of voices, the serenity of the ocean. Far away, Sabina's high-pitched voice rose in the air:

"Buenos días Su Señoría, Mata Tiru Tiru La. Qué quería Su Señoría, Mata Tiru Tiru La."

And then, Leandro's voice, casual and brusque, and faintly sarcastic:

"Your mouth, Maya."

"My mouth?"

"It is odd. It always looks as though it were about to swallow a sacred wafer."

Maya laughed, a short full laugh. And then, again, the seabirds, the sea, the wind. I buried my face in the sand and felt the warm, dense mass of heat, the salt, the foretaste of laughter. I thought, The harlequinade is not yet over.

Part Two

one

Dusk. A taste of fog in the air. Tall, swaying poplars. The shadows of seabirds. Mist. Fireflies.

I was standing on the large outdoor terrace, looking down into the orchards, the fountains. Far away, the blue of the sea was fading; the dunes rose slowly to crests, dipping, crumpling. I thought, It's nearly evening. Soon they will leave their dressing tables, their mirrors, and appear at the top of the stairs, magnificently dressed, gleaming. If one did not know them, one could not help but think that they are virtue personified. They will glide down the stairs and make their usual elegant entrance. I shall look up and they will say, Good evening, my dear; and our smiles will widen; we shall drink martinis and talk briefly about anything trivial. Eight o'clock will strike. Dinner will be announced. We shall dine outdoors, on the terrace. We shall glide into the gardens and take our seats opposite one another, among candles and flowers, and become absorbed in the food and wines. Dinner will be superb, as usual, and a little too long, a little dull. Laura will stroke her cheek wistfully and gaze at us out of her great brown eyes. She will say, Cards? Charades? Someone will answer, Anything you like, my dear. Later we shall wander back to our own rooms and pause in front of the dressing table, frowning slightly at the weary reflection in the mirror. We shall undress, lie down in bed, without moving, without thinking, and turn out our lights.

I started out of my musing as Maya appeared on the terrace. She was dressed in one of her white silk gowns and her hair was elaborately piled up on her head, gleaming, exposing her graceful white neck and shoulders. She walked quietly toward me and stood beside me, her elbows on the balustrade. She remained thus a long time.

"Look," she said, at last, "the vanishing forms and colors."

The air became dense as the last glow of the day waned and night rose toward the sky. The lethargy and melancholy of the fading day touched Maya's face. It clouded. The light went out of her eyes as though she, too, were slowly sinking into eclipse. When she spoke, her eyes were vacant, brooding.

"Night will come," she said, "much against our will."

We remained on the terrace a moment longer, breathing the air that was full of fog, watching the sea, the crested dunes, the vast silent acquiescence of the sky. And then Maya said:

"I'm going for a walk."

"Shall I come with you?"

She shrugged and wandered away, as though her mind were dwelling on something quite different from her ordinary affairs. I followed her as she moved across the gardens, the shrubs, the flowering trees with vines climbing them, toward the gravel path where the flat green lawn turned into a rocky footpath that led to the main road.

We made our way in silence toward the town, the sound of our footsteps echoing throughout the deserted streets. A solitary sound. The town was quiet. The lights had just come on and there was a moist warmth in the air. I threw a furtive glance at Maya as we walked on toward the square. Her face was pale and mournful under the glow of the street lamps. She seemed to have sunk into one of her inexplicable moods, and for an instant I caught a glimpse of the remoteness, the arrogance, in her features. I thought, We ought not to be silent.

"Maya," I said, and smiled at her.

She returned a wry smile.

"I rather wanted to be alone," she said.

She walked on abstractedly. I flung a quick glance at her eyes, her grimness, the sad corners of her mouth. I smiled and slipped a hand under her arm, and I felt her warmth. We were silent for a while. Then she said abruptly:

"We are idlers. All of us."

"Yes," I said.

"Passers-by."

"Yes."

"We exist. Like light exists. Uncorrupted. I suppose it is quite natural. One does not have to ask oneself any questions."

"No," I said, "I suppose not."

She was looking at me intently. Her eyes were like two small brown wounds on her face. She gazed at me curiously a moment longer and a soft gleam came into her eyes.

She said, "Julyan tells me that I exist solely in appearance."

"A ghost," I said, smiling.

"At times Julyan goes rather too far," she said vaguely.

She had raised her head and was looking into my face. Her eyes were dim, mild, serene; like the sea is serene after the wind has fallen. I looked into the depths of those eyes. I thought, A shell.

We fell silent again and continued to walk across the

deserted square, among dimly lit cafés and rising shadows. On the far side of the square we came upon the village church, pale, purposeless, austere, against the soft glimmer of dusk.

"Ah, the village church," Maya said sweetly, as though a curious impulse had come upon her.

"Yes," I said.

"Let us go to Him."

"To whom?"

"The Old Sentinel who dwells within."

I thought, A confrontation, and followed her as she quickened her step and plunged into the dimness, the gaunt ugliness of the brown-washed walls, the turbid light. Maya dipped her hands in holy water and moistened her face and throat.

"My face is hot," she said.

We slackened our pace and glided down the aisle as though we would never reach the end of the deserted church. The altar was still far, far away, and there was a blur before my eyes. I thought, The bread of life. As usual, I experienced the uneasy sensation that the air was hardly fit to breathe.

"Like the smell of a cellar," I said.

"Incense," said Maya, "and flowers."

Flowers, all over the room, carefully arranged in porcelain vases. A glimpse of flowers beyond the window. A patch of sun between the curtains. Old, colonial furniture. A dusty piano. Leather-bound books. Maya was sitting on a corner chair, quietly, with eyes downcast and lips set. Her face looked like a chalk drawing and her lips were quivering. She said abruptly, "Must we stay? I don't want to stay. I don't want to see her." "Hush," Nanna said, "above all, there must be no fuss." "I don't want to see her," Maya said, staring fixedly at the toes of her shoes. "I haven't seen her for years. I haven't seen her since she ran off with the schoolmaster." "Hush," said Nanna. "Well," Maya went on, unperturbed, "she did run off with the schoolmaster, didn't she?" "Hush. Let's not lose our sense of proper behavior." "I haven't seen her for years. She wasn't even allowed at Papa's funeral. They said, Off with you, and off she went. Why must I see her now?" "It's different now," Nanna said. "She and the gentleman have been married. A natural length of time has elapsed since your poor papa's death. Besides, she is your own blood. You have an obligation to fulfill in the eyes of the Lord. The Lord wants us to put aside our false pride and be merciful." "I don't care. She is ugly and wicked and I hate her." "Hush," said Nanna, "hush." Silence. A sense of dimness, anguish. The sound of footsteps. A door, opening. I raised my eyes and looked at her. She was standing in silence, beside the schoolmaster, looking down at our faces with moist eyes and parted lips. She was thinner than I remembered her. Her face was bony, nostalgic, somewhat familiar.

Her left eye was twitching. "Nanna," she said, "you were sweet to bring the children." I looked at her face, her blankness, her twitching eyelid. I thought, She ought to have said My child, rather than The children; after all, I'm only a cousin; not even a blood cousin. But then I felt Nanna's brisk nudge on my ribs and quickly stepped forward, kissed her on the cheek, and called her Auntie. I turned toward the schoolmaster, curtsied, and flung a quick glance at him. He wore dark-brown braces and there was a faintly aromatic fragrance about him. Maya was standing, grim and motionless, on the far corner of the room. Her mother walked over to her and remained silent a long, long time. Then, suddenly, she smiled her old smile, leaned forward, and held her in her arms. "You were sweet to come," she said. "Won't you give your mother a kiss?" Maya raised her face and looked deeply into her eyes. The tiniest smile lifted the corner of her lips. "I'm afraid I don't quite know what you mean," she said courteously. "I don't know who you are. I have never seen you before."

The sound of Maya's laughter broke the silence and echoed throughout the deserted church. I raised my head and looked at her. My eyes had grown accustomed to the dimness and I could distinguish her face quite clearly. Her lips were quivering as she laughed. She felt the weight of my look upon her and flung a quick glance at me.

"I laugh," she said, "for the pleasure of laughing."

Her laughter broke off abruptly: the impulse was dispelled. Her face grew pale and she bit her lips. She became abstracted and intent, as though a rare, bewildering feeling had arisen within her, as though she had become absorbed in a role of humility and self-condemnation. I thought, Guilt, perhaps.

Maya moved onto the front pew and knelt down. I stood next to her, stiff and silent, unwilling to commit myself, yet feeling somewhat burdened and responsible. The smell of incense was everywhere. Beyond the pillars, the altar was dark. Vast. Imponderable. Maya's hands were clasped and her lips were moving silently. Her cheeks were flushed.

One stroke sounded from the church's clock. I tiptoed to where Maya was kneeling with her back toward me and laid a finger on her shoulder.

"The half-hour," I said. "We ought to go back to the villa."

She shrugged and got up gloomily.

"I'm willing," she said.

We walked noiselessly out of the church and made our way in silence to the villa.

two

A faintly golden villa overlooking the sea. A rose garden. Dim. Fragrant. A foghorn in the distance. Sweet dusk. White, blurred faces, like clouds of mist. A taste of lemon peel on the lips.

I thought, A summer bazaar.

Julyan, in a low, hurried voice, as he leans toward her with pale eyes and trembling lips: "There is a bruise on your lips." Maya starts. She turns around to look at him, and seeing his face above hers, the look in his eyes, she finds nothing to say. She presses her face into a large bunch of white flowers, unable to prevent a furious blush, and smiles faintly, a little breathless.

Silence.

Laura, laughing, as they wander about the gardens together: "You are perfectly charming. Why do we never quarrel?" Juan-Luis smiles. An expert smile, sensual, sheepish. He squeezes the small, jeweled hand that is resting on his arm and kisses a cheek that smells faintly of sweet violets.

Darkness under the cedar trees.

Coco, tightening her hold on Sabina's hand and stroking it gently, a look of anguish in her bright observant eyes: "You've had a very tiring day. You tire yourself so easily. And then you cry in your sleep. You cry a lot in your sleep. You have been sleeping badly these past few nights." Sabina tries to pull her hand away and fails. She smiles sweetly. She twists her fingers and digs her nails hard into Coco's hand.

Laurels. Primroses.

Leandro, alone at the other end of the pergola, with his back toward us: ". . . high summer."

Fog.

Pablo, in a low whisper, as he leans forward to light my cigarette: "Liliana." I turn toward him and rest my hand on his arm. I smile at him, a soothing smile, full of gladness. His hand closes suddenly upon mine. His eyes are no longer idle; his mouth droops a little. "I want you," he says, "always."

And that was how it was.

Summer. The air full of orange blossoms and dew. Love, a rare sweetness. Restlessness. Laughter. The sea, the foghorns, the dunes. A delicate balance, weakening. A touch of fantasy. And us. All of us. Nothing more.

three

Dinner, on the terrace, under the flowering trees.

We glided into the gardens, pausing briefly to inspect the brilliant array of silver, candles, and flowers. We sat under the ivy-covered pergola, sipping our cocktails, arguing back and forth across the table, laughing. Silver lids were removed and silver spoons expertly handled, as course after course was presented, admired, savored. Chilled consommé. Breast of pheasant in a sherry sauce. Watercress. Chambolle-Musigny. Lemon soufflé made of the thinnest air. From the depths of the gardens, the quiet, restrained rhythm of a mulatto's guitar; his fingers upon the strings like moth-soft wings.

Afterward, Laura rested her chin on her small, jeweled hand and gazed at us out of her great brown eyes. From the distance her face was an exquisite fragile mask. She threw us a little wistful smile, a foretaste of boredom clinging to her lips.

"Cards?" she said with an absent air. "Charades?"

"Anything you like," said Juan-Luis, leaning forward to light her cigarette.

"We may, of course, retire to the library. And politics."

"Or Schopenhauer."

"Or poetry."

"Or chess."

I tipped my glass and glanced at them, their affected nonchalance; their limp smiles; their faces that merely simulated a dull enthusiasm. I thought, It's no use.

It was then that Leandro told us about the game.

"Rather a treacherous game," he said, smiling, "like quicksand."

He rose and advanced toward the end of the table with a purposeful stride. We sat back and waited, a little awed, drawn into an involuntary curiosity. We glanced at his eyes, his mouth, as though the fairness of his patrician head were, in itself, sufficient. He walked on, without hurrying himself, amused by the searching expressions on our faces, our silence, our willingness to be made into his accomplices.

"Leandro," Laura said, to her own surprise, "you have kept us waiting."

His glance crossed hers. Her eyes were anxious but determined. It appeared that she would not have a moment's rest until she plunged into the wonder of that which awaited her. Leandro's eyes wandered coolly and he smiled, an indolent smile that flattened his lips.

"My dear Laura," he said, "what is a game to you?"

"You aren't fair," she said. "You must tell us."

He did. He spoke calmly, with the slightest trace of sarcasm in his voice, and we immediately recognized the detachment, the carelessness, the scattering of words like puffs of smoke. We listened to the words flowing past, the sounds that rose above the night.

"A game of self-abandonment," Leandro said, "in which we shall cease to be ourselves; we shall renounce our tastes, our wills, and engage in a contest of chance. A game in which we shall risk our freedom."

We burst into laughter. The first since Leandro had spoken. Dry laughter, like a faint flicker in the darkness. It broke off abruptly. Once again, the sweet-scented stillness. I thought, An old dream, sinking back upon itself; upon the outer edge of consciousness.

"You may, of course, refuse to play the game," Leandro said, with that languid, vague attitude that we accepted as irresponsibility. "Yet you might enjoy saying yes."

A long silence followed. There was a sense of anguish, of resignation; a feeling of tumbling into the shadows. Leandro leaned forward, his hands flat on the table, his shoulders hunched. He regarded us in a quiet, almost benign, manner. And waited. He said at last:

"Well?"

The evening seemed suddenly to awaken. We emptied our glasses and sat quite still, our faces turned toward Leandro, and looked at him with bewilderment. We spoke abruptly, with firm, resolute voices that sped through the blackness and wavered into silence.

"We'll play."

"Ah, well," Leandro said, a half-smile on his lips, "you must learn the rules."

four

A raffle.

A game without sense, or purpose, or reason. A game like a legend: absurd, invulnerable; like a battle we would fight against ourselves, tearing ourselves from the calm, almost indifferent stillness of the evening to plunge into a rather bewildering awakening.

There was such laziness, such tenderness, in Leandro's voice as he told us the rules that we felt a surge of exultation sweeping toward us as we sat, close together, in the dimly lit pergola. Then his voice died out and he smiled faintly.

We returned his smile, already accustomed to the idea of falling into a moral complicity based upon laughter and gaiety. The inevitable was about to happen and we prepared ourselves to risk anything. Everything.

The rules were quite simple.

Those of us willing to raffle ourselves off would come forth and deliver our offering. Chance would rule thereafter.

Thus the prizes were chosen.

Sabina was first. She offered herself with sulky indolence. She stood before us, rolling a golden strand of hair round her finger and smiling her loveliest smile.

"My virginity," Sabina said in a triumphant tone, and her upper lip curled over her tiny white teeth.

We stared her full in the face: her youth, her freshness, her childlike sensuality. We were stunned. She was standing very erect, gowned in a cloud of white sequins and silk, and her eyes were like water. She folded her arms; her hands began to stroke her shoulders, and then they slid downward to the hollow under her arms, and around her small, white breasts, gently, gently. Her cheeks were slightly flushed and her eyes were glowing as though she were frightened by her own audacity.

"Lovely," Sabina said.

Coco was watching her from beneath her eyelids. Her eyes were dark, sluggish, as though she were possessed by a gripping force, as though she were in pain. Her mouth was wide open, but the words would not come. She repressed the anxiety, the contemptuous thoughts that were no doubt invading her mind, and remained humble and silent. She dropped her eyes and stared at the toes of her shoes, tight-lipped and a little dazzled. I thought, Alas.

The evening was gray, smooth, transparent. There was a sense of fatigue, of shadows, gliding slowly toward the end of the lawn, retreating into the distance. I felt my eyelids growing heavy, my lips growing numb. I thought, I must not go to sleep.

I rose, stood before them, and made my offering as Sabina had done: quite simply, without ceremony. I smiled. I laid my hand upon my abdomen and stroked it gently, with the tips of my fingers, there, where the child was asleep, clutching the darkness.

"The child," I said, with a short, dry laugh.

They turned their startled faces toward me and regarded me in silence. It made me dizzy for a moment. I looked at the tiny lanterns swaying to and fro along the hedges; at the shadows, grouping, regrouping, suddenly dashing across the darkness. I thought, It makes my eyes ache.

I flung a quick glance at Pablo and caught but a glimpse of the wreckage. He was sitting quite alone, his shoulders hunched, his fist clenched upon the table. His face had changed. It was sullen. His mouth was quivering, as though a flood of anger had risen to his lips. I looked at his broad shoulders, his eyes, his youth, constantly on guard. I thought, He will never forgive me.

The evening was calm, impersonal, with the faraway stillness of things that belong to the past. Beyond the dunes, the rich cadence of the sea, rising, falling, gurgling into silence.

Leandro rose. His shadow was huge and misshapen against the ivy-covered wall. He was leaning forward, crouching a little, his hands in the pockets of his white linen trousers, a negligent smile on his lips. He made his offering in a light, indifferent voice that made no attempt to conceal his profound amusement.

"The lower depths of hell," he said, "in an embrace."

Thus, Sabina personified Purity; I, Fertility; and Leandro, Damnation.

And we engaged in a raffle.

five

They were silent.

Their faces were smooth, expectant; their glasses were no longer clinking. They were looking at Leandro with curiosity and a mild complacency, as though they had managed to forget themselves and were allowing themselves the luxury of a little distraction. I thought, His will is their will.

"Chance," Leandro said, "will determine our pleasure. Or downfall."

They exchanged amused glances and looked at Leandro's hands, as they swiftly shuffled the cards, again and again.

"The cards bear your names," Leandro said, a thin smile clinging to his lips, "a matter beyond dispute."

He shuffled the cards once more, slowly, deliberately, taking pleasure in delaying the decisive moment. At last he laid the cards face down on the table.

A silence fell. All faces turned toward Sabina. She was bending over the table with an air of perplexity, her face like a cloud of mist. She remained motionless a moment longer, smiling with her eyes closed, her hands folded as if in prayer.

Her hand dropped abruptly and her fingers fumbled along the table. They felt their way blindly; they passed close to the cards, hesitated, withdrew. They stood still, finally, and she held the chosen card between thumb and forefinger. Her eyes opened wide. She parted her lips and read the name without lifting her head.

"Juan-Luis."

He raised his head and his body started with a sudden thrill. He drew a deep breath. His eyelids folded over his eyes.

Sabina glided quietly toward him, her cheeks flushed, her face half-hidden by her long strands of hair. He saw her come and rose in silence, a little drunk, a little breathless; barely conscious of her presence except as a startling, almost convulsive feeling that had suddenly sprung within him.

He reached out a hand and smoothed her hair back over her cheeks. Her face, smooth and fragile, reappeared beneath her blond shocks of hair. Her eyes were shut. He brushed her eyelids with his lips.

She turned her face toward him, without looking at him. She buried her face in her hands and whispered:

"Juan-Luis."

I thought, Sleepwalkers, and rose to my feet, swaying a little. I held myself very stiffly and gripped the edge of the table. I stood motionless, listening to the distant hum of the sea, the wind, the crickets that lay hidden in the grasses. A warmth rose in the pit of my womb, creating a small tremor which ran all the way up my body; then the little waves ceased, and the child found refuge in my own stillness.

Darkness filled my eyes. My fingers wandered about the table, groping their way blindly. They dragged on for a while, stiff and heavy, and then they slowed down. My fingertips rested upon the nearest card. No. The farthest. No. The nearest.

I lowered my head and opened my eyes. I stood perfectly still, holding my breath. My heart was thumping. I spoke his name, almost silently:

"Julyan."

I caught a glimpse of him: a tall, distant figure, with drooping shoulders and dangling arms. I walked across the dewy lawn, the blood throbbing at my temples and wrists, and stood before him, motionless and silent, a mere presence merging into the night; a drifting shadow.

Julyan's eyes narrowed. He stretched out his hand

and laid it on my shoulder. A smile rose to his lips: a smile that gave nothing of himself, that awaited nothing.

"Ah," he said, with a short, dry laugh, "the rightful owner."

I leaned forward and kissed him. He took me in his arms and kissed my temples and ran his finger over my cheek. After a moment he moved away. His hand tore itself away from my shoulder and fell heavily to his side. His smile slowly died away. I thought, An ebbing tide.

Leandro's laughter startled me out of my abstraction. He was slowly walking back toward the pergola, the last chosen card in his hands. His shadow crept slowly across the ground, as though it had wrenched itself free of his body. Each stride he took seemed to push the shadow from behind: a smooth, unbroken flow.

He stood under a slant of light, his face and hands in full view. His eyes glittered and he uttered a roguish laugh. He spoke her name quietly, as though the vividness of the first impression had exhausted itself:

"Maya."

He went to her at once, creeping slowly and silently across the garden as though he were gathering himself to leap forward. He leaned over her and took her head between his hands, burying his fingers in her hair.

Maya's eyes opened wide, enormous. Her mouth was twitching a little. She darted her head from side to side, her eyes filled with gloom and bewilderment. I thought, Like a cornered animal.

"Come, my dear," Leandro said. "It will be a long journey to hell."

She sat, upright and silent, staring into his eyes with an expression I had never seen before. Her lips were trembling. He moistened them with the end of his tongue, and then he took hold of her mouth; he slipped his tongue between her lips, and pressed onward, clumsily, greedily. She made no attempt to resist him. Her body went limp and a shudder ran through her long, handsome limbs.

The night was filled with rustlings, with moods. Far off, the sea was motionless, the wind had fallen. The sky was, like the ground, dark and tranquil, and a smell of laurels and smoke filled our nostrils. I thought, Caged. All of us. The winners. And the losers. And the scapegoats. And those who have taken the hindmost. And those who have taken nothing.

And then Coco rose from her dark corner, and the words came tumbling out of her mouth.

"Enough," she said, "the game is over."

She walked over to Sabina and gazed at her with a warm, embracing glance. Sabina was sitting beside Juan-Luis, pressing close against him. He was stroking her head as it lay on his shoulder and breathing into her hair.

Coco moved forward with an oddly awkward gesture and grasped Sabina by the arm.

"Come," she said, "you are very fatigued. You need your rest."

Sabina drew back, slowly rousing herself from her lethargy. She blinked and looked morosely about her. Her eyes met Coco's and she smiled a sweet, angelic smile.

"Will you come?" Coco said, a little out of breath.

Sabina did not answer. She was rolling a strand of hair round her finger and tugging it, smiling ecstatically. Suddenly her mouth drooped and her eyes closed; her head sank once more onto Juan-Luis's shoulder. She whimpered a little.

"Sabina," Coco said, "you will have one of your beastly headaches in the morning."

Sabina was looking at her, open-mouthed and listless. She seemed to ponder for a moment. She rose with an effort, sullenly, abstractedly, stumbling a little. Coco held out her arms to her, her eyes full of longing, of understanding. Sabina's head rose stiffly. She reached out a hand and quietly grasped Juan-Luis's hand.

"Take me away from here," she said.

Coco's face drained of color.

"No!" she said violently.

She turned to Juan-Luis, whose existence could no longer be ignored. She said, without looking at him:

"Leave her alone."

He looked her in the face as he stood beside Sabina, his arm around her shoulder, waiting in silence. There was neither friendliness nor anger in his look. Only a gleam of awareness, a slight sense of embarrassment.

Coco turned toward Laura with the air of someone who has suddenly discovered the closest, most intimate ally:

the only vulnerable one. "Laura," she said, "tell him to leave her alone."

Laura smiled. She touched up her elegant headdress, smoothing the curls back over her forehead. She threw back her head and smiled her thin-lipped, celebrated smile.

"My dear Coco," she said sweetly, "you flatter me. I have absolutely no claim on his time."

Coco's lips were livid and trembling. She looked around her with an expression of confusion, almost of animal fear.

"Sabina," she pleaded, "tell them, tell them."

Her words sank back into the darkness. Juan-Luis put an arm around Sabina's waist and drew her away. She went of her own accord, pressing close against him, her face half-hidden by her hair.

I looked at Coco, at her wrathful, averted eyes, her anguish, her clumsiness. I thought, The longest vigil.

"She ought to have known," I said to Julyan. "Don't you think?"

"It doesn't concern me," Julyan said dryly.

He drank up his brandy and said, "What's the time?"

"Midnight."

"Are you tired, Liliana?"

"A little."

"Would you like to retire?"

"Not quite."

"Well," he said, getting up, "whenever you say. I shall be in the bar."

six

The evening was calm, tender, a little extravagant. Pablo emerged from the garden and bent over me. He held me close, almost fearfully, without a word.

"You little traitor," he said finally in a quiet voice.

I raised my head and saw his face, his discontent, and felt the strange intimacy of his embrace. I smiled and held out my hand to him. He seized it, and I felt the warmth of his skin clinging to mine.

"What is happening to us?" Pablo said, and there was anguish in his eyes. "We are drifting."

"A form of self-protection," I said, my lips against his face.

His hand was stroking my face, wearily, as though it were at a loss.

"Come," he said abruptly.

"Where to?"

"Back to Lima. With me."

"When?"

"Tonight. Now."

I smiled, gently, and shook my head. He was watching me attentively, and I saw the candlelight flickering in his eyes, the fearful expectancy, the traces of reproach in his face.

"No," I said.

"Why not?"

"It's late. I am tired."

I rested my head on his shoulder and his warm, familiar smell filled my nostrils. I closed my eyes, suddenly fatigued.

"Liliana," Pablo said, "I want you."

He was kissing my ears and temples and breathing heavily into my hair. His mouth was warm, urgent, a little clumsy. I thought of red roofs, of geraniums in the window boxes, of the sun flickering on Pablo's brown, naked body. My mouth opened under his.

"I want you," he said, and his eyes were hard.

"Yes," I said.

"The child, too."

"The child?"

"Yes."

"The child is Julyan's."

"It is not!"

"It is, Pablo, it is."

"He won the child in a raffle. Is that what you are trying to say?"

"Nonsense. The child is his."

"By deed of chance."

"Really, Pablo," I said, laughing.

He edged closer to me, groaning a little. I slipped my arms around his neck and pressed close against him and began to fumble with his clothes. With mine. He shook his head and drew away, dully, as though he were tearing himself away from oblivion, from sleep.

"Not here," he said.

"Where?"

"Away from him. In Lima. Come back to Lima with me."

"No."

"Please, Liliana."

"No."

He drew away from me and passed his hand over his face, slowly, uneasily. His eyes were remote, bewildered; they were looking at me as though they attempted to break through a barrier. A sad lingering look, like a false sense of hope, like absence.

"I see," Pablo said at last. "You refuse to come with me."

"It's past midnight," I said. "I am very tired. I want to sleep."

"With him. In his bed."

"I am exhausted. I want to sleep."

"You sleep in his bed. Don't you?"

"Yes."

"A thing of habit, I suppose."

"Yes."

"You sleep with me, too."

"Yes."

"Why?"

"Please. No more questions."

"You sleep with me. Yet you refuse to leave him."

"Them."

"As you like. Them. You sleep with me. Yet you refuse to leave them. Why?"

"Pablo. Please."

"You are too unfair. The three of you."

He suddenly drew me toward him, almost brutally; his arms tightened around my waist and his head dropped to my shoulder. He buried his lips in my hair. His voice was almost a sob.

"Please, Liliana," he said, "please."

I reached out and touched his face. I put my arms around him and kissed his face, his lips. His mouth was clinging to mine, restless and confused, leaving a taste of absence and salt on my lips.

"Dear Pablo," I said.

There was silence. He looked down at his hands, then smoothed his clothes, mechanically, fastidiously, fumbling with one of his cufflinks that had come loose. Then, he took my hand and slowly raised it to his lips.

"Wednesday?" he said.

"Yes," I said, "of course."

He made a curious, awkward movement toward me. Then he abruptly turned away, and I watched the nape of his neck, his broad shoulders, his arms hanging loosely by his sides, as he slowly made his way up the driveway.

seven

Julyan was alone in the bar. His face was shadowed, beautiful. He was leaning against the bar, his arms folded, his eyes half-closed, in a withdrawn, negligent attitude. I said, "Hello, Julyan," and stood quietly beside him, feeling his uneasiness, his perplexity, his silent, staring eyes. It was a moment of strange intimacy, brief, unknown, a little terrifying. It caught us unawares and it lasted long enough for us to stand, face to face with one another, with a smile of hope, solicitude, resignation.

The moment passed. I held out my hand and he

poured some brandy into a glass and handed it to me. I took a sip. My lips felt dry. There was a warm, sour taste in my mouth.

"You should have told me about the child," Julyan said.

"Yes," I said, "I suppose."

"How long have you known?"

"Not long."

He was watching me through half-closed eyelids. His eyes were uneasy and a little mistrustful, as though he found it hard to look me in the face. He was standing motionless, immersed in the darkness that stretched out before him. I thought, A player's king.

"You don't mind having the child?" he asked abruptly.

"No," I said, "of course not."

There was silence. The blood was throbbing at my temples, and I felt a little weak at the knees. I leaned against the wall and held myself very stiffly.

"And you?" I asked. "Do you mind?"

He drew back with a start. He looked at me, scowling, and remained at a loss. His eyes were almost hostile. He gripped his glass and twirled it in his fingers, eyeing it gravely.

"There are things that one can't do anything about," he said.

I dropped my eyes and held out my glass and he poured a little more brandy into it.

"I suppose the child is an absolute certainty," Julyan said.

I raised the glass to my lips and emptied the brandy into my mouth. It was warm and burning as it went down my throat.

"Is it?" Julyan asked.

"Yes," I said.

"Have you had the usual tests?"

"Yes."

"What was the result?"

"Positive."

"I see."

The lamps shed flashes of light through the pine trees, suddenly whitening Julyan's face, flickering, darkening. His eyes were dazed, wide open, as though he had awakened with a start. He was watching me with a quizzical expression.

"When will you have the child?" Julyan asked.

"Sometime around the end of winter."

"Rather a long wait, isn't it?"

I remained silent, calm. Far off, the sea was completely at ease, the sea-wind was cold, brisk. Julyan lit a cigarette and blew a large cloud of smoke.

"You've rather sprung the child on us," he said, and his voice was unusually quiet, composed.

He said no more. He reached out and touched my face in a light, caressing gesture. I looked at his face, his smile, the sad intensity in his eyes. He appeared to have engaged in a struggle to overcome a tumult of conflicting emotions without losing his composure. He seemed to be sinking down into a lightless pit from where he would emerge, blinking, exhausted, gripped by a disconcerting blend of forces. He would neither accept nor repudiate the child, but reconcile himself to its existence, its singleness of purpose, while simultaneously dismissing from his mind any rupture or change in our present situation. Momentarily, at least. I thought, An emotional standstill.

I remained silent and looked steadily ahead of me, at the pale, somnolent light that lingered between the pine trees. There was a sense of stillness, fatigue. A series of fragmentary recollections began flooding my mind, as they always did, obscurely, a bit incoherently, like a search for things that no longer exist, like shadows swirling into the wind.

Purple shadows, quivering in the night. Tall, lean shadows, plunging into the middle of the dance floor. A jazz band, shrill, metallic. A small corner table. Three drinks on the table. A blaze of light, followed by blackness. I raised my eyes and looked at them as they slowly glided past the table. They were dancing, quietly, in silence, on the far corner of the dance floor, pressing close against one another. Julyan rested his handsome, dark-haired head against hers and buried his lips in her hair. Maya stiffened a little and made a feeble attempt to hold herself aloof, but his arms tightened around her waist, knowingly, without haste, with a slow, sensual motion that drew her to him, weak, unresisting, her face drained of color, her eyes wide open, dazed, her breasts and thighs pressed close against him. I lit a cigarette. I smiled at the bartender, jovial, aloof, and said, Straight up, and watched him pour the martini into my glass. I blew a large cloud of smoke and looked at the dance floor without lifting my eyes. They were moving in close spirals, spinning, swirling, no longer conscious of themselves, possessed by a gripping force that thrilled their senses, absorbed and consumed their thoughts, their willfulness. She had closed her eyes and laid her head on his shoulder. Her lips were trembling, and there were deep shadows under her eyes. I thought, A sleepless night. The last broken sound of a guitar died out, and they slowly glided into silence. They remained standing still, in the darkness, in the middle of the dance floor, as though they no longer had the strength to move, and I recognized the blank, defenseless expression on their faces, the somnolence, the awkwardness. She threw back her head and looked fixedly into his eyes, pale, calm, a little baffled, and seeing their look, I dropped my eyes. I sipped my martini, and watched their shadows.

"Liliana," Julyan said, "what is the time?"

"Midnight," I said.

The night was filled with rustlings, with fog. There

was darkness beyond the pine trees, and a smell of laurels and smoke filled the air. Far away, the sea had awakened a little. We could hear the soft lap-lap of the waves, the distant sound of a foghorn.

"It's late," Julyan said. "We ought to retire."

"Yes."

"Where is Maya?"

"I don't know."

"I expect she is still out in the garden."

"Yes," I said, "I suppose."

"Well," Julyan said, "Leandro's game has lasted long enough, don't you think? Let's go and fetch her."

eight

Her face was a whitish blotch. Her mouth was soft, feverish. She had loosened her hair and it was tumbling all over her face and shoulders. Her white silk gown had slipped off her shoulders and bared her breasts. She was kneeling on the ground, beyond the laurels, where the ground was dark, warm, dewy. She was kneeling quietly, in silence, face to face with him, her body soft, limp, at rest.

Leandro's face was quite close to hers. His smile was blurred and a little drunk, as his eyes devoured the purity and nakedness of her fair, swollen breasts. His hand was outstretched upon her flesh. A sculptor's hand: free, impudent. He laid his hand on her breast and caressed it with long, gliding strokes, and I caught a glimpse of his eyes, his yearning, his remoteness, the inexplicable quality of his whim that could be measured only in terms of willfulness.

Leandro moved closer to her. Quietly. Without hurrying himself. He held her warmth between his hands: felt it against his own. And then he slowly bent his head and his lips tasted the moist nakedness of her skin, her drowsiness.

I turned my face toward Julyan and saw the look in his eyes, his clenched teeth. I drew a deep breath and laid my hand on his arm. He shook it off and flung himself forward, his face pale and convulsed. He thrust Leandro aside and planted himself before Maya as she knelt huddled over the tall grasses.

"Maya," he said, in a low heavy voice, "that's enough."

Maya was silent. Her face was withdrawn, ambiguous. Julyan clasped her head in his hands and looked deep into her eyes. There was an awkward touch to his gestures, his familiarity.

"Maya," he said. "Liliana and I have come for you. We have come to take you away. With us. Haven't we, Liliana?"

I looked up, smiled at him, and lit my cigarette with trembling fingers. A moment passed. The air was filled with stillness, with smoke. My head was whirling a little and my knees began to tremble. I leaned backward and rested my head against the ivy-covered wall.

Leandro's soft laughter roused me from my weariness. I turned around to look at him, and I was startled by the gay exaltation in his eyes, his carefully controlled aloofness, his hunger. He remained standing on the far end of the pergola, on the spot where Julyan had jostled him. He was brushing the pine needles off his sleeve and smiling with the air of a man who has nothing more to do but wait.

"It's no use," Leandro said, "each game has its own rules."

The blood surged into Julyan's face. He clasped Maya's head in his hands and buried his fingers in her thick, luxurious hair. He took her face by the chin and forced her head up with a furious, resolute air.

"Look at me," he said. "Look at me."

Maya was jerking her head from side to side, her face half-wild and beautiful. She uttered a cry and her hands caught his wrists in an effort to push him away and free herself. Julyan drew her to him so savagely that a convulsive spasm rippled down her body. Her eyes filled with tears of pain and her head hung, heavy and unresisting, in his hands. A flood of bitterness rose to his lips and he spoke to her as I had never heard him speak before. Icily. Brutally. In a low, heavy voice. Through half-closed lips. And then I watched his hand rise. I followed its awkward movement as it rose, curved, hesitated in mid-air, and came down upon her face with a dull thud.

A silence fell. Julyan dropped his arms. He clasped his hands tightly and closed his eyes, as though the vision of her stunned, humiliated face still lingered in his eyes. His head had sunk between his shoulders, as though he longed to sink his senses into the refuge of his own abstraction. I thought, A fugitive.

Maya's face was hidden in the shadows. I could no longer see her eyes: only the nape of her neck, her hair tumbling over her face, her whiteness.

Leandro's laughter was soft, dull, barely audible. His shadow stood out, thin and flat, against the dimness.

Far away, the bare sands, the sea, the smell of seaweed and salt, the trees swaying gently in the breeze. There was a faint fragrance of rain; a sense of loneliness and sleep.

I raised my head and saw Julyan's face above mine. His face was gaunt, drained of anger.

"Liliana," he said, "it's late."

"Yes," I said.

"Are you tired?"

"A little."

"Would you like to retire?"

"Yes."

"Come," he said.

I followed him across the dimly lit gardens, through the darkness, the stillness, the passing shadows.

nine

A villa at rest. Elegant. Remote. Asleep. Perched upon cragged mountain rocks that sloped gently down to the sea. Outside the window, the emptiness of the sea, a bleary sky, the sound of the waves breaking lightly on the beach.

Julyan had thrown his jacket and necktie on the bed and was standing silently by the window. He remained thus a long time, his shoulders hunched, his forehead against the windowpane: a blank, dismal figure, like the center-point of darkness.

"Liliana," he said at last, "are you asleep?"

"No," I said.

He walked quietly toward the center of the room, where I lay outstretched on the bed. The bedclothes were chill. I watched the red glow of his cigarette as it rose to his lips.

"Liliana," he said, and all his anguish and wrath flooded into his voice again, "it must have been one of her moods. One of those ugly, fateful moods of hers. It must have been quite painful."

"Yes," I said, "I suppose."

"She is her own mood," he said. "She can't help herself. She sinks into those turmoils of hers until she is drained. And then she loathes herself."

"Yes," I said, "I know."

"It has happened before. Many times. It happened again tonight. It comes. And it passes. Like a storm passes."

"Yes."

"And now it's over."

He fell silent. He sat down on the edge of the bed, beside me, and passed his hand slowly over my face and hair. I placed my hand on his and stroked it gently. I took his cigarette away and crushed it in the ashtray. There was a long agonized pause.

"Liliana," Julyan said in a faltering voice, "I want to ask you something."

"Yes, Julyan?"

He was stroking my face, smoothing my hair. He grasped my hand and rested his forehead against it. His fingers were cold and clammy and his forehead was burning.

"Please go to her," Julyan said.

"Now?"

"Please."

"It's very late."

"It's not quite dawn. She is never able to sleep before dawn. Even though her mood leaves her, she is unable to disengage herself completely. The brittleness remains. So does the loneliness. She can endure anything but loneliness. Please go to her."

I groped for my wrap in the darkness. I put it on and it felt soft and warm against my skin. I walked back and forth and around the bed, feeling the softness of the carpet under my bare feet.

"My slippers," I said.

Julyan gripped my hand and slowly raised it to his lips and I felt his moist, feverish mouth against my wrist. A moment passed. I stroked his head gently, absently, and stood beside him, motionless and silent, very much at a loss. And then, for one brief moment, I caught a glimpse of a ludicrous image of myself: a tall, thin, impotent archangel bending stiffly over the awe-stricken head of mankind. I thought, An onlooker, and a shudder ran up my legs, into the pit of my stomach. I gathered the wrap tightly under my chin and withdrew my hand from Julyan's grasp. I slid my feet into the slippers and walked out of our room into the dimly lit corridors.

There was light under Maya's door. I lingered a few moments outside. I heard her walking about the room, humming a little tune. I heard the sound of running water. I knocked.

"Maya," I said, "may I come in?"

The door opened slightly and she let me in. She had flung her white silk wrap over her shoulders and her hair was tumbling down over her face and shoulders. She was barefooted, as usual.

"Liliana!" she said, and leaned over to kiss me.

"Are you alone?" I said.

"My flowers and I," she said as I followed her into the room.

The room was full of flowers, carefully arranged in earthenware pots and porcelain vases. Hyacinths, orchids, gardenias, orange blossoms, narcissus. A strong, over-sweet fragrance pervaded the room, spreading into the farthest corners.

"Maya," I said, "this is outrageous. Laura's head gardener will be very cross."

"There will be other flowers," Maya said as she glided into the bathroom.

She slipped off her wrap and stepped into the bathtub and sank into the warmth, the blueness. She rested her head against the white porcelain and shut her eyes. She folded her arms over her breasts and massaged her throat and shoulders, moaning a little, as though she were in pain. Her face was pale, languid, and there were circles under her eyes.

"Maya," I said, "there are shadows under your eyes."

Her soft, marvelous face drooped a little. She lay there, very quiet, immersed in water: a floating, solitary lily.

"Leandro was rather a brute," she said, and a smile lifted the corner of her lips.

Then, quite suddenly, her face changed as though a new, unfamiliar emotion had stirred within her; as though she were reluctant to emerge from her torpor to face its strangeness. She cupped the water in her hands and moistened her face and lips.

"Is Julyan very angry?" she said without looking at me.

I lowered my eyes and looked away. I remained silent, staring at my hands and fingernails. My hands felt enormously heavy and damp and a bit in the way.

"Liliana," Maya said, "is Julyan very angry?"

"Yes," I said, "I suppose he is."

"Is he very, very angry?"

"Yes," I said.

She rested her head against the white porcelain and sank deeper into the warmth of her bath. Her skin was so translucent that I could see the blueness of her veins all over her throat and breasts. I thought, A bed of nettles.

"So futile," she said vaguely, "so utterly futile."

"What is futile, Maya?"

"Julyan's anger. Us. Everything."

"Why?"

"It all dissolves into a huge, smooth-faced shadow."

Shadows, beyond the pine trees. The chill of dusk in the air. A graveyard. Desolate. Deserted. Maya's burning hand, holding mine. We found our way in silence, hurrying along the rows of tombstones, the sound of our footsteps muffled by the dry leaves. I said, "Nanna will be cross if we stay away too long." Maya was sullen, listless. She let go my hand, knelt on the ground and pressed her face against the stone marking the grave. She whispered, "Papa," and began to sob. Her face was hidden by her hair; her shoulders were shaking with awkward little jerks. "Papa," she said. She kept stroking the bare gravestone with her hand and saying, "Papa," "Papa," as though to herself. She suddenly raised her head and got up. She walked away with tight lips and clenched fists. I caught sight of what she was doing and cried out, horrified, "Maya!" She started and turned around with a quiet, resolute air. There was a strange look in her eyes, anxious, yet unrelenting. Her mouth was quivering. She dropped her eyes and moved away swiftly, scurrying around from grave to grave, gathering armfuls of flowers. I waited silently until she returned, carrying the flowers in her outstretched arms. Her face was very white. The tears had dried on her cheeks. "Thief," I said. Again, the look of anguish in her eyes, the quivering lips. "Hush," she said without anger. She bent her knees and crouched down in front of her father's grave and carefully spread the flowers around it. She took a crumpled flower and twirled it in her fingers. "They will look nice in the light of morning," she said. "Thief," I said.

"Liliana," Maya said, "will you fetch my wrap?"

I held it out for her and she stepped out of the bathtub, put the gown on, drew it tightly about her, and went on into the bedroom. She leaned over the narrow brass bed and pulled down the bedclothes. Her dolls were lying on their backs against the cushions, wide-eyed and red-lipped. She eyed them tenderly and stroked their blond hair.

She stood in front of the mirror and contemplated herself with a quizzical smile, her head tilted a little to one side, as though she were looking at something much farther away than the forlorn, oval-shaped face that stared back at her.

"At times I would like to take my reflection off the mirror," she said.

She stood in front of the mirror and contemplated her-glance crossed mine, and her eyes were like a windless night, like stillness.

"Liliana," she said, "you ought to have told us about the child."

"Well," I said.

"How long have you known?"

"Not very long at all."

She left the mirror and walked slowly toward me and stood before me, waiting. And then she stepped over the invisible threshold and said, "Please. May I?"

She leaned forward and pressed her face against my abdomen, against the faint vibrations, the inscrutable darkness, the sense of wonder. I looked down at her handsome head, the curve of her stooping shoulders, her eyelashes.

"Julyan's child is inside," she said, pressing her face closer against my abdomen.

"Yes," I said.

"Why! It's soundless."

"Yes, rather. A simmering murmur, at most, if one listens through a stethoscope."

"Does it keep quite still?"

"Yes. Quite."

"Does it feel lovely?"

"Well, yes. Actually, it doesn't feel very much like anything."

"Is it quite heavy?"

"No," I said, with a laugh. "It is weightless."

"Yet it exists," she said, and her voice was tranquil, empty.

She rose and slowly moved away. She bent her head over a large terra-cotta vase and buried her face in the blossoms and inhaled their fragrance.

Outside the window the sea stretched out into the distance, leaden, serene, with only an occasional burst of foam. The sun was not yet bright beyond the haze, but light was beginning to filter through the curtains.

"Maya," I said, "it's very late."

"Don't go," she said. "Please stay. I'll play the guitar for you."

"No," I said, "it's terribly late."

"Don't go. Please don't go. Stay."

"No," I said, and slowly turned around and made my way to the door.

I heard the muffled sound of her footsteps as she walked across the room; I felt her cold fingertips upon my wrists, her breath brushing my face.

"Please, Liliana," she pleaded, "stay. I'll play the guitar for you. I'll play *Sandunga*. Please stay."

Her voice swirled in the air, dreamily, hazily, like a wisp of smoke.

Ay, Sandunga,
Sandunga, mamá por Dios,
Sandunga, no seas ingrata . . .

I lifted my head and saw her face. I saw her eyes. The yearning. The fatigue. The shadows about her mouth. I thought, An eclipse.

"No," I said, "no, Maya."

And then she drew a deep breath and her voice vanished into the shadows. She lifted her head and her face came out of the darkness like a patch of gray. Her eyes were wide, enormous. Her lips were twitching a little.

"Please!" she said in an imploring voice. "Don't leave me."

I lowered my eyes and slowly shook my head. I moved noiselessly toward the door and looked around me, at the gray hazy light that lingered on Maya's head, on her lips, like mist.

"Good night," I said. "Sleep well."

She was leaning against the narrow brass bed, her arms hanging loosely by her sides. Her eyes were shining, but her face remained calm. Her voice was light, mild, matter of fact.

"It's almost dawn," she said, and a faint smile lifted the corners of her lips.

"Yes," I said, and smiled back at her.

I opened the door quietly, fumbling a little with the doorknob. And left her.

ten

Dawn, almost.

The curtains were drawn and there was a faint smell of wet foliage, mist. I walked to the window and opened it, gently, noiselessly. Light was beginning to filter through the haze. The sea was blotted away. I could see an occasional glint of water beyond the bare sands, the crests of the dunes, the rocks.

"Julyan," I said, "it's dawn."

He was sitting up on the edge of the bed, motionless, unsmiling, his shoulders hunched, his eyes half-closed. I walked across the room and stood facing him, stooping a little.

"Julyan," I said.

He raised his head and looked at me and his eyes were still, inscrutable: a curious blending of serenity and fear.

"Liliana," he said, "did you see her?"

"Yes," I said.

"How were you able to find her?"

"There was light under her bedroom door."

"Was she alone there?"

"Yes."

"Was she all right?"

"Well, she was very tired. She will be all right by morning."

"She was very cross, I suppose."

"No. Not cross. Only tired."

"She was not cross, then?"

"No."

"Did she say anything about—him?"

"Nothing."

"Nothing?" he repeated with a bewildered air.

"No," I said. "I imagine it will all end in that."

He heaved a deep sigh and his head sank between his shoulders. His eyes were shut. His lips were quivering. He spoke my name, again and again, and his voice failed him a little; he was quite out of breath. I laid my hand on his head and stroked it absently. Without tolerance. Without reproach. I stood beside him, motionless and silent, and stroked his forehead and temples, and I felt his temples beating steadily against my fingertips.

"Julyan," I said, "let's not talk any more. You look exhausted. You ought to try to sleep."

He rose with a listless air. He walked away from the bed and began to undress with a dull look in his eyes and a distraught expression on his face, as though he were unable to shake off the fresh anxieties, the seed-bearing thoughts. I saw his dim, hesitant silhouette, the purity of his nakedness, his face, his wide staring eyes.

I drew a deep breath and closed my eyes. Julyan crossed the room with his slow, silent stride. He leaned over me and pressed me to him and kissed me lightly on the lips. A sudden thrill ran up my body, and I leaned against the narrow brass bed, breathless, dazzled, lost.

Julyan lay on one side of the bed and I heard the subtle sound of the springs. His head sank on the pillow and he closed his eyes. I watched his face from beneath my eyelids, his fatigue, his pallor.

I slipped off my robe and lay down beside him and drew up the bedclothes and we remained outstretched on the narrow brass bed, inert, oppressed, our bodies barely touching. I thought, Like two wooden statues.

"Liliana," Julyan said, "will you switch off the light?"

I did. The room was bathed in a flat, sallow light that was rather cheerless.

"We shall leave in the morning," Julyan said, his voice heavy with sleep, "and we shall take her with us."

There was a long moment of stillness. I remained motionless and silent, staring into the shadows that were still lurking in the farthest corners of the room. I closed my eyes and my head began to whirl. In my mind's eye, Maya's face was clearly visible, her eyes were dark, enormous, her lips were quivering. She was leaning against the narrow brass bed, her arms hanging loosely by her sides. "Please, Liliana, stay." I saw her face, again and again, coming out of the darkness like a patch of gray. "Please, stay." I felt her cold, clammy fingertips upon my wrists, her lips against my face. "Stay. Stay. Stay. Stay."

There was grayness all around, everywhere. A soft light was beginning to filter through the curtains. I shut my eyes tightly and pressed my hands against my closed eyelids. Slowly and tortuously sleep was thrusting its way through the depths of my conscious mind. I thought, I'm not my sister's keeper.

And slept.

eleven

They found her at dawn.

The Coast Guard patrol had been circling the waters off the bay during a routine early-morning assignment.

They had spotted her at once, delicately poised over the clear bluish water: a small, wavering shadow drifting away into the current.

They had known it was one of the villa's guests because they had seen her before. Many times. Many summers. It had been a habit of hers to dive off the rocks and swim in the wan half-light of dawn, into twilight, into morning, there, where the water was peaceful and tranquil, and the current was swift.

I awakened with a start as the boat's distress siren rose out of the deep quiet and filled the air with a dry, dusty sound. A long silence followed. And then, again, the short, dry sound, rising and falling and sinking into silence. I turned my head and flung a quick glance at Julyan.

"Julyan," I said, "we must hurry."

He was adrift in the slow motion of sleep. Haste and conflict were gone from his face and he was breathing peaceably, serenely, his face turned away from the light, the uneasiness, the sense of intrusion.

I slid out of bed and flung a robe over my shoulders and hurried out of the room, out of the villa, across the gardens, into the bare sands, to the beach.

Laura and Leandro were already there. They were standing side by side, awkward, irresolute, incredulous. We were the only ones: Laura, Leandro, and I. All the others were absent.

I moved closer to them and rested my hand on Laura's arm.

"Laura," I said.

She held out her hand with a faint, dismal smile. She was grim and rigid in her purple dressing gown and her nighttime makeup. Her eyes were shielded by enormous sunglasses.

She whispered, "My God," through half-closed lips.

And that was all she said.

Leandro's face was drained of color. His lips were livid. And so was his shadow, gray, as it slanted down into the bare sands.

"Leandro," I said.

"They did all they could," he said mechanically.

"Yes."

"The undertow was quite strong."

"Yes."

"She wasn't out too far. She must have lost her strength while swimming back in."

"Yes," I said, "yes."

The air was chill. I clutched my dressing gown close under my chin and slowly looked away. I looked all around me. Everywhere. I looked at the bleached sands, stretching out into the distance. The glint of water, beyond the cliffs. The willows. The shadows. The mist. There was a smell of seaweed and salt in the air. A dry taste in my mouth. A taste of violets and dust.